The Birthday Books

The Birthday Books

JOANNA LILLEY

HAGIOS PRESS

A CIP catalogue record for this book is available from
Library and Archives Canada

ISBN 9781926710334

Edited by Tina Dmytryshyn.
Designed and typeset by Donald Ward.
Cover art: painting by John Brocke titled "Shelley" from the
collection of the Tom Baker Cancer Centre, Foothills Hospital,
Calgary. Used with the kind permission of Anna Gardner.
Cover design by Tania Wolk, Go Giraffe Go Inc.
Set in Minion Pro.
Printed and bound in Canada at Houghton Boston Printers
and Lithographers, Saskatoon.

The publishers gratefully acknowledge the assistance of the
Saskatchewan Arts Board, The Canada Council for the Arts,
and the Cultural Industries Development Fund (Saskatchewan Department of Culture, Youth & Recreation) in the pro-
duction of this book.

HAGIOS PRESS
Box 33024 Cathedral PO
Regina SK   S4T 7X2
www.hagiospress.som

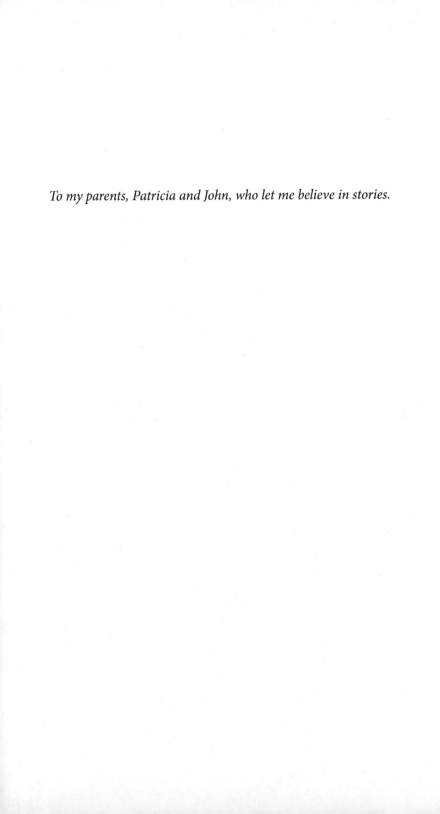

To my parents, Patricia and John, who let me believe in stories.

Contents

The Birthday Books

LIZZIE LEANED HER BICYCLE AGAINST THE BACK OF THE LITTLE blue house she rented and stood to sniff the sharp scent of the logs she'd spent the weekend splitting and neatly stacking. She didn't know why she always left it so late, why she never did anything until she had to, like an obstinate child. It wasn't because she didn't want the cold to come, because she did. She loved the long white winters of the Yukon; it was when she felt most Canadian.

In the kitchen, the answer phone light was flashing. She never had difficulty ignoring the phone when it rang, yet she could never pass by that slow red blink. She pressed the pulsing button with a firm finger and went to the fridge.

"Darling."

Her mother. Who never left a message, only the intolerant click of a receiver being replaced. Lizzie closed the fridge door so she could pay attention to her mother's voice, still unsaturated, as she had once heard her mother say, by the corpulence of the Canadian accent, even though it had been more than thirty years since she'd left England.

"Darling. Your father's died," her mother said in quick, lean tones. "You'll be getting some paperwork from his solicitor."

When a feeling came, it wasn't sadness or regret, it was the spine-straightening sensation of relief. There was no longer any possibility that she'd see her father again.

It was almost ten o'clock in Halifax. Her mother didn't appreciate telephone calls late in the evening but this was a crisis. Or not. According to her mother, it was only a matter of paperwork. So there was no rush.

As she moved about the kitchen, peeling garlic and tearing basil for a pasta sauce, Lizzie glanced every now and then at the phone as if to catch it in the act of looking at her. Only after she had finished eating and washed and put away the dishes did she pick up the receiver and start to dial.

"Mom. It's Lizzie."

"You'll have to sort out the sale between you. I don't want anything to do with it."

"Telepathy is yet another skill you didn't pass on to your daughter," Lizzie said.

"His house. He's left it to you and Luke and some money. Not a penny for me, but then I wouldn't have taken it anyway."

"Luke won't want the house."

"No," agreed her mother, and Lizzie knew at once that she had spoken to him already, had called him first. Luke, Lizzie's brother, was working in London. Each time she heard him speak, he sounded more and more English.

"There's no point seeing it," her mother said.

"No," Lizzie said. Her father's house in Victoria. By the ocean.

"You can pay people to clear it out."

"Yes."

"You won't want anything. You're not a pack rat."

"True," Lizzie said. Her mother would be visualising Lizzie's first apartment, in Toronto. Lizzie hadn't had much to put in it and she'd liked it that way. She'd decided only to acquire objects she would keep for the rest of her life. After Toronto, she had moved steadily west, dangerously toward her father, then north as if a magnet had flipped and repelled her from him. Her mother hadn't visited any of these other places, as if her elastic would snap if she stretched any farther west.

"The money will be useful," her mother said. "You won't have to live in the middle of nowhere any more."

LIZZIE LEANED BACK in her seat on the Greyhound bus and swirled a thumb on her iPhone until she found the music she wanted. The Waifs started. She liked listening to Australian music because it had nothing to do with her. She leaned back in the seat and looked out the window. Yesterday, at last, it had snowed. The aspens and willows were bare of leaves, but with snow in their clefts and fissures they no longer looked nude. She was glad to be going by bus. A couple of years ago she'd flown south to Vancouver around this time of year. It was plus eight when she left and minus twenty-eight when she returned a few days later. She'd been cold the entire winter.

The Waifs ended and Coloured Stone began. Now that her father was dead, it was safe to see how he had lived after he left them. She was going because she wanted to, not because her mother didn't want her to. She wasn't that childish. The journey to Victoria would take one day: twenty-one hours and thirty minutes, including the ferry. She had music and movies and no regrets about not bringing a book. The scrape of paper between finger and thumb gave her blackboard shivers and she hated the way you had to hold a book in your hands.

She didn't know where her father had got the idea she liked reading. Every birthday since he'd left them, just before she turned eight, he'd mailed her a book. *The Magic Faraway Tree* was first. She'd been so excited when the parcel arrived but when she saw it was a book she'd squeezed her eyes closed to keep the tears inside. She didn't even take it up to her room but left it among the magazines, ornaments, and ashtrays on the sideboard where she knew it was easy for things to become lost.

The next birthday her father sent her *Five Children and It*, and the following year *The Secret Garden*, just more class-ridden English crap she'd seen on television. It wasn't as if her father was even English. He was an English lover, an anglophile, a word Lizzie hated because it made her picture her parents having sex.

Next, a box set of Susan Cooper books with spooky covers. He never sent books to Luke, only money, and at Christmas he would give her a reprieve and send her money, too. Even though Lizzie had never once thanked him, he was as persistent as *Reader's Digest*. The last book he'd sent her, just this year, was a hardcover edition of *Jane Eyre* of all things, with his usual inscription as if he was the bloody author. She'd given it to the Salvation Army along with a shirt she'd bought that was too big for her.

A black bear, two moose, two deer, and more bison than she could count. She wouldn't have seen any of them if she'd had her head down reading.

Further south, after the snow thinned to cotton grass, the deciduous leaves were red as well as gold, and eventually there were tulips and pansies in flower beds. On the ferry she stood on the deck breathing salt into her bloodstream until the vehicles started to drive off.

SHE'D ANTICIPATED something Georgian — a hipped roof, sash windows. But his house was white, a composition of rectangles with large windows as blank as primed canvases.

The solicitor had given her a key. There was no reason not to go in and help herself to the inevitable PG Tips in his cupboard. The solicitor said he'd been jogging in a park. A woman had been with him but he was dead before he reached the hospital. A heart attack. Lizzie wondered if the woman had been English. There was an uncle somewhere too, her father's brother, who was arranging the funeral and who might contest the will for all she knew.

Lizzie walked up stone steps and put the key in the lock.

She opened the door slowly, ready to cough from book dust,

inhale the mildewed arguments pressed between the pages.

If anything, she could smell furniture polish; she couldn't even see any books. None piled on the dining table that you had to move every time you wanted to eat, or against the basement door because it kept swinging open, or heaped all over the floor to trip you up.

Shaking off her shoes, Lizzie went further in, the soles of her feet warmed by a red and orange rug that looked African.

The walls in the open living space, she began to see, were covered with bookshelves reaching like ladders from maplewood floors to high white ceilings.

Wooden floors and shelves, wooden tables and chairs and ochre and terracotta couches. It was beautiful. It was tidy.

This was where he had brought all his books to live. The home he had given them when he took them from Halifax, leaving empty shelves that her mother never refilled and a couple of years later got a man to take down in the process of redecorating. Even though the new paint was thick, Lizzie had still been able to feel the indentations where the shelves had once been screwed to the walls.

Upstairs, there were hardly any books; there were views. Through the bedroom window, smudged by mist, was a pastel sketch of chalky ocean and peaks. A scene that would change on other days to an oil painting, charcoal sketch, or watercolour.

She looked around the room. There was a book on one of the bedside tables and she went over to see what it was. *The Winter Vault* by Anne Michaels. Lizzie flipped it over to scan the back. At last he was reading Canadian authors. She put the book down and sat on the bed.

She remembered how once when she was about six she had been wriggling into the warmth between her parents in their bed. Something hard had jabbed into her back and she had cried out. Waking at the sound, her mother shouted at her father to get his bloody books out of the bed. Bloody in English was worse than bloody in Canadian, Lizzie knew even then.

She had laid there between them, wanting to say sorry to her father for getting him into trouble but instead she'd pretended to fall asleep. If she had said she was sorry, her mother would have called her Daddy's girl again, and somehow that would have been worse.

She stood up from the bed, not bothering to tug out the wrinkles she'd made her in father's bedspread. There was one small bookcase in the room and she went over to it, angling her head to see which books had received the honour of being kept in his bedroom.

She crouched and hooked a finger to lever out a spine that looked familiar. It was *The Magic Faraway Tree*. Three children sitting on a broad beech branch. She lifted the cover. "To my darling Lizzie," said the inscription. "I'll be with you in spirit on your eighth birthday. I love you. Daddy."

It was the actual book he had mailed her. She recalled the inscription, how she had thought it meant he would turn into a ghost and visit her on her birthday and how she had waited.

She looked along the spines on the bookcase. There was a copy of every book he had sent her while she'd still been living at home, as if he'd bought copies so he could read them at the same time as her. Well, she certainly hadn't played along with that little game.

How could these books have got here?

Still holding *The Magic Faraway Tree*, she sat back on her heels and lifted a page, careful not to scrape her fingers on the paper and set her teeth on edge. The first few lines of the story were familiar. Perhaps she had read a little of it after all.

Her mother must have mailed the books back to him, perhaps with a note to say Lizzie didn't want them. Or more likely with no explanation. Had her father thought that Lizzie herself had returned them? It had never occurred to her to send them back. It was more that he was sending her the wrong message, not that she didn't want a message at all.

She placed the books in a pile on the floor then picked up the stack with both hands. If the Susan Cooper box set counted as one, there were ten; one for each year between his leaving and her leaving. She carried the stack out of the room but at the top of the stairs turned back and added *The Winter Vault* to the pile, careful not to dislodge the receipt he had been using as a bookmark.

In the kitchen, she put the books on the table and filled the kettle. Her iPhone rang just as she found the teabags.

"I've been trying to call you. You're not at home," her mother said.

"No."

"I had to call your mobile. I hate how they make one have to shout."

"Yes," Lizzie said. Even though cell phones hadn't even been invented when she'd left England, her mother refused to employ the North American term.

"I see," her mother said.

"See what?"

"You're there, aren't you? I knew you'd go."

"What do you mean?"

"I don't know how you could, Lizzie, after what he did to us." The kettle on the stove started to squeal. "What's that dreadful noise?"

"The kettle," Lizzie said, turning off the heat. "I'm having a cup of tea."

"I don't suppose he has a proper kettle like normal people." By proper, she meant a plug-in. By normal, she meant English.

"Did you," Lizzie said, "send him back all my birthday books?"

"Of course I did."

"But they were mine."

"For goodness' sake, you didn't want them. And I certainly didn't want bits of him in the house. You didn't exactly rip them open with excitement. You barely touched them. All I had to do was Sellotape the flap and stick them back in the mail."

"Return to sender."

"Exactly."

Lizzie opened the box of PG Tips, dropped a teabag into a mug and picked up the kettle.

"Lizzie?"

Lizzie poured hot water onto the teabag.

"You are not going to live in that house," her mother said. "I won't have it. Lizzie, did you hear what I said?"

Lizzie ended the call and switched off her iPhone.

She didn't bother drinking the tea. She went from room to room, looking along each bookcase, head tilted. In the fiction section, near the staircase, she removed the last book her father had sent her and took it to the kitchen. Letting the table hold it for her, she sat and opened it to the first page and read the first line: "There was no possibility of taking a walk that day."

Rearranging Rainbows

RUBY SHOVED HER FEET INTO HER OLD PINK CROCS READY for the walk to the washroom trailer. She never used her own facilities if there was an alternative. Opening the door, she stopped; there was no washroom trailer. They'd left it in Vancouver to save on gas. Because it was 2,697 kilometres to the vast metropolis of Whitehorse. She'd counted every milepost as they'd driven past trees, trees, trees that grew scrawnier and blacker as they went north. They reminded her of Bob when he'd been on the tanning bed too long.

It had been Marco the ring master's idea. They'd all felt sorry for him because of his dad dying, so they went along with it. And now he was talking about going on to Fairbanks so they could be the first circus to travel the entire Alaska Highway.

Before she closed the door, Ruby looked across at the elephantine RV that Marco had inherited. Even though it was nearly lunchtime, the drapes were drawn. Marco was keeping the drapes closed on himself, too; whenever she asked him how he was, all he said was, "Good, thanks."

As usual, Marco had parked to the right of her and Bob. On the left were the Canolli Family and their cloud of poodles. Circus people loved to think they were free spirits, unbound by the routines that fettered house dwellers, yet wherever they went they always parked their homes on wheels in the same formation. They might as well be living in a subdivision.

Ruby shut the door, walked along the corridor they called the dining room and squeezed herself into her bathroom. Trailer bathrooms were clearly designed by men who forgot that women had to turn round in order to perform. Sitting at last on the toilet, Ruby arranged her bath robe over her legs to hide her thighs. She sighed and let herself give in to it; her dream of a nine-to-five office job. Her eighty grams per square metre fantasy. Her rat race reverie.

She stood up and flushed.

Being in a circus was like being a member of the Royal Family. Except in the circus you couldn't abdicate. Whatever your mom and grandma did, you did, too. Artistes didn't have career changes and a career break was exactly that; a fall could be the grand finale of your airborne employment. Once your waist and hips conjoined you worked off-ring. What other options were there when you'd never had a normal job?

HERE SHE WAS, lifting linen, pinching polyester in a clothing store. She'd gone for a walk along the slow wide river and meandered onto Main Street. She touched only the classic suits, the designs that suggested you had more important things to care about than your figure. This was absurd; she was supposed to be looking for leotards and tights.

Ruby turned away from the clothing racks and walked quickly outside, feeling a jiggle in her flanks and belly. Back by the river, she stopped to watch the water gliding by. It looked thick, gluey, as if northern water was a different element, as if she could jump in and go under and still breathe.

Ruby knew where she was really heading. She'd seen it on the free map at the visitor centre. A Staples store. She trotted toward it along the dusty riverside path.

Inside Staples, she bought herself a block of rainbow Post-its. She put the plastic bag with her treasure in her jacket pocket and kept her hand wrapped around the package all the way home.

IT WAS TIME FOR HER daily visit with her eighty-two-year-old grandma, Emerald, who had driven all the way here in her own RV. A convoy of one because she'd insisted on sleeping by day and driving by night in the hope of seeing the northern lights. Except as they travelled north the nights got lighter and shorter and she didn't catch even a flash of the aurora borealis. Here in Whitehorse, sometimes Ruby saw her during the night, wandering between the trailers looking up at the pale sky.

RUBY KNEW SHE WASN'T going to be able to use the Post-its. But she still tried; she stuck a fluorescent orange one on the mirror to inform Bob, who was soiling the trailer facilities and taking his time about it, too, that she was popping out to see Emerald.

"For Christ's sake, woman," he said when she returned. "Why d'you have to go scribbling on bits of paper when we live within spitting distance of each other? And that colour gives me a headache."

"You never say that about my outfits," said Ruby, squeezing in behind the table. She ripped a Snickers wrapper and took a bite.

"The colour of your get-ups is the least of my concerns," said Bob, taking the iron out of the closet. "I'm more worried you're going to burst out of them."

"Perhaps, Bob," she said, after another bite, "I eat because I'm unhappy."

"It's Roberto, not Bob. What have you got to be unhappy about? You're in the star act." He leaned his face close to the iron and turned the dial. He was too vain, even inside his own trailer, to wear glasses. "Is it the change, Ruby love?" he murmured as he floated his violet cloak onto the ironing board. "You're getting to that age, after all."

"Thank you for calling," Ruby whispered so quietly she was really just miming the words. "Have a great day."

Ruby was standing backstage, peeking at the audience. She let the heavy curtain fall back and went over to Marco, the creases in his red tails and black trousers as neat as folded paper. He gave her a smile but she could see his heart wasn't in it. Emerald started to pick lint off Ruby's leotard, as if they were chimpanzees grooming each other. She almost expected Emerald to pop the lint in her mouth.

"Twins on?" Ruby said to Marco. She was just making conversation. She knew exactly what was happening on the other side of the curtains by the music the band was playing: Romulus was throwing knives at Remus and Remus was throwing fire at Romulus.

Marco nodded.

"The sad truth, Marco," said Ruby, adjusting a strap and marvelling that there had once been a time when she hadn't needed a bra, "is we can't say we're not living the lives we imagined for ourselves because we've never been able to imagine anything else."

He raised an eyebrow.

Emerald stopped, apparently having run out of lint to pluck.

"The thing is," continued Ruby, "if we don't do something soon we're not even going to have this. There's hardly anyone in the audience."

Marco spoke softly. "I'm not like him, Ruby," he said. "I never will be."

Bob was always saying that Marco wasn't a shadow of his dead father, the Fabulous Fabio Fraccio. Ruby defended Marco every time but she couldn't deny Bob was right when he said Marco spent too much time alone in his trailer.

"Just because you call yourself fabulous," Ruby said gently to Marco, "doesn't mean you are."

On a furtive trip to Staples three cities ago, she'd spotted Marco with a bag in each hand coming out of a store that sold model kits. Miniature aeroplanes, boats, trains. She'd never said anything, least of all to Bob, who would only use the information as gunpowder to fire the last of Marco's self-esteem beyond reach once and for all. As long as Marco wasn't sniffing the glue he used for his models, it was none of her business. Anyway, who was she to talk, what with her futile fetish for stationery.

"You know what, Marco?" she said. "Driving the Alaska Highway would have been a great publicity stunt if it hadn't been so expensive. We've got to catch up with the twenty-first century before it's the twenty-second. Online bookings for a start."

"What's this?" laughed Bob, approaching with a smile as fake as his tan. "I thought old-fashioned pens and paper were more your thing, Ruby honey. Our camper looks more like Staples every day. I keep expecting to wake up to find my breakfast made out of origami."

"Pens and paper have their place but — " started Ruby.

"Just about every place in our place," quipped Bob.

Ruby glared at Bob as Marco looked courteously away.

Emerald stroked Ruby's arm and gave her a kiss on the cheek. "Don't break a leg," she said.

That's what Ruby's mother, Sapphire, used to say to Ruby when she was a child and about to run through the curtains into the ring. Ruby and Emerald looked at each other. Sapphire had broken more than a leg. Ruby hadn't even made it to double figures when Emerald had had to become a mother all over again.

The curtains parted and Romulus and Remus ran toward them. Remus was holding one hand in the other and there was blood seeping through his fingers. "Cut me once more, you fucking idiot," he said to Romulus as they ran past, "and I'll set fire to your RV."

"We need," Ruby said, turning back to Marco, "a website. And proper marketing. You didn't even phone the papers to tell them we were coming up the highway did you?"

Marco winced.

"Not now, Ruby dear," Bob said. "Marco's on."

"Shit," said Marco and swept through the curtains into the ring.

"Poor Moping Marco," laughed Bob. "He'll never be as Fabulous as Fabio."

"Leave him alone," Ruby said. "We can't all be perfect like you."

He looked at her. "I've been thinking, Ruby, dear," he smiled. "Perhaps a bit of a break would do you good if you're depressed."

"I said unhappy, not depressed."

"You could take a trip with Emerald while we're here. Pan for gold. Take in a cancan show."

"You can do the act on your own, eh?"

"Actually, I was thinking of Maria. She's showing a lot of promise these days."

"She's showing a lot of cleavage, that's for sure."

"Not now, Ruby, dear. There's no time for that. Come on, we're on."

STANDING ON THE TRAPEZE PLATFORM, Ruby scrutinized Bob, trying to see beneath the tan, the eyeliner, the foundation, to the man she'd fallen in love with. But she'd discovered long ago that wiping off his makeup was like wiping a misted window. He was as hard as glass and just as transparent.

As he started the routine, she glanced down. Good. Not many kids in. Here Bob came, her scrawny gibbon. Funny how it took more concentration to get it wrong than to get it right. It was a struggle to stop her muscles responding to the double-tonguing trumpet and the lift of Bob's limbs.

All she had to do was raise her arms a quarter-note early after her double flip. Bob's wrists were on their way but a skin's width too low. She flew on and under him. Down, diving, dancing with gravity. Landing in the net didn't hurt; she'd fallen enough times as a child to remember how to arrange her limbs.

Bob, evidently, had forgotten.

Her landing had been silent. His was counterpointed with cracks. She heard them over the audience's gasps and the cornet's crescendo. That hadn't been the plan. She'd only wanted to knock him off his not so metaphorical perch.

The musicians lowered their instruments as she moved as easily as a spider across a web to stand over him, knees soft to absorb the net's bounce. "Bob?" He wasn't moving. "Bob, are you okay?"

"It's Roberto, not Bob," he grimaced, opening his eyes.

Emerald was first up onto the net. Ruby hadn't realized she still had it in her.

"Best to keep quiet," Emerald said to Bob. "Save your strength."

When the men lifted him off the net, his roar reminded her of Leonardo the Lion. She missed poor Leo. She wished the animal rights people hadn't made them give him to a zoo.

Ruby ran alongside the stretcher. "I'm sorry. It was my fault."

"Damn right it was your fault. You're too fat. It's screwed up your trajectory."

She stopped running and stood to watch the paramedics carry him away.

RUBY RUSHED TO CHANGE into the most normal clothes she owned. She didn't want people to stare at her in the hospital. Blue jeans and a pink t-shirt would do, even if they did feel like they'd shrunk in the wash. But as she stepped up into a red truck with Fabulous Fraccio's Circus painted in gold down both sides she shook her head and laughed; she might as well not have bothered changing; she stuck out like the proverbial sore thumb.

"I'M SORRY, BOB, I don't know what happened," she lied as she sat down by his bed at the hospital.

"It's Roberto," he said, "and you need to take a look at yourself. You've lost your focus and you've lost your figure."

Ruby looked at the hospital bedspread draped over the cast on Bob's leg. It was a nice colour, almost the same pink as her t-shirt.

"You've got to sort yourself out," added Bob. "Things can't go on like this."

"You're right, Boberto," said Ruby, standing up. "Things can't go on like this."

THERE WAS A KNOCK on Ruby's RV door. She shoved the Mr. Big she was eating under a seat cushion and called, "Come in."

"How are you doing, darling," Emerald said. She switched on the kettle and took a couple of mugs out of a cupboard.

"I should be doing that," Ruby said.

"I was thinking," said Emerald, once she'd got the teabags and milk ready, "perhaps Bob is right."

"I can't stop eating. I don't know what's wrong with me," Ruby said.

"Not that," Emerald said. "You're gorgeous. Curvaceous. Though you might want to watch your cholesterol. What I meant was, maybe you should have a break."

"I haven't got much choice now, have I?"

"There's something the house dwellers say," Emerald said. "A change is as good as a rest." She took a piece of paper out of her pocket and unfolded it in front of Ruby. It was a newspaper clipping. "This is a nice town," Emerald said. "Take a look at this."

TEN MINUTES AFTER Emerald left, there was a quieter knock at the door.

"Come in," Ruby said. This time, she left the Mr. Big on the table. The door opened tentatively. "Oh hello, Marco. Come on in. Sit down."

He had every right to fire her and for good, not just out of a cannon.

"You're right," he said, sitting down. Tonight, everyone was right. "We've got to catch up with the twenty-first century," he continued. "I was thinking, while Bob's out of action, I mean Roberto, we could do some planning. A business plan. Isn't that what we need? You could be my manager, executive director, vice president. Whatever you want."

"It's too late, Marco," sighed Ruby.

"Oh," Marco said. He clasped his hands together in his lap and the slenderness of his fingers made Ruby wonder if he could have been a pianist or perhaps a surgeon.

"I don't mean for the circus," Ruby said. "A business plan is a great idea. You should do it. I mean I think it's too late for me."

RUBY WATCHED A GOLDEN LEAF float past on the river. Even though it was only August, the leaves were already changing colour. The circus hadn't made enough money to be able to go on to Fairbanks and now they had run out of summer. It was time to return south. They were already taking down the big top. From where she was standing across the park, it looked like a mushroom someone had trodden on. They never did it right, even though she'd told them enough times.

She pulled her fleece over her red shirt and made her way back. Her lunch break was over. Making her way through the store to the staff room, she stopped to put back a folder that had fallen to the floor, then stood rearranging its companions. Someone had placed purple next to yellow. Colours should whisper to each other, not shout.

Sylvia on the till was watching. "I dunno, Ruby," she called. "You'd rearrange the colours in a rainbow if you could reach them."

Ruby smiled. In her old life, she would have retorted that she could reach them, all she needed was a trapeze. But Sylvia didn't know about that life. Only the manager knew and she'd agreed not to mention it, not until Ruby's trial period was over. Another two days and Ruby would know if she had a future in paper and pens or if the only thing she was any good at was being a monkey's mate. It was Emerald she had to thank. She was the one who had torn out the Staples recruitment ad, helped her find a room without wheels to live in, and now Emerald was about to go south without her.

THE STORE DOOR OPENED and Sylvia rushed to help the man coming in. Crutches, a leg in plaster, an arm in a sling.

"You still like to make an entrance, I see," said Ruby when he saw her. He had a speck of glitter trapped in the wrinkles under one eye.

"You weren't hard to find," Bob said. "You've got Marco's whip wrapped around your finger, duping him into writing you a reference."

"I'm working," said Ruby, glancing at Sylvia, who was looking as entertained as a kid in a ringside seat. "I can't talk."

"That didn't used to stop you," Bob said. "Nice," he added, propping himself up against the counter and looking round.

"It's a lot better since Ruby started," Sylvia said, missing the sarcasm. "She's got us organized."

Bob's smile stretched his lips but didn't disturb the rest of his face. "Come on, Ruby, dear. It's time to come back. We're leaving town tomorrow."

"Maria isn't showing as much promise as you'd hoped?"

Bob adjusted his crutches. "I was only kidding," he said. "Okay, I was being a jerk. If I hadn't said such nasty things to you, you wouldn't have lost your focus. Come on Ruby, sweetie. You and I are magic together, you know we are. Don't you miss it? Flying through the air?"

The last person Ruby would admit missing the circus to was Bob. "This is my job now," she said.

"I don't understand you," Bob said. "You'll never make it as a house dweller. And in Whitehorse of all places?" He laughed and this time his whole face joined in.

Ruby opened the door for him and waited until he had gone through.

Once the door was shut, Sylvia turned to look at Ruby.

There was no more reason to hide the truth. "I've run away from the circus," Ruby said.

Sylvia looked confused.

"Yeah, I know." Ruby smiled. "Wrong way round, right?"

ON RUBY'S LAST TRIAL DAY, the manager handed her a white box as she stood at the till. "We don't encourage staff to receive personal mail," she said.

"I'm sorry. I'll tell" — Ruby looked to see who it was from but it didn't say — "I'll tell whoever it's from not to do it again."

Her name was written on the top of the box with a calligraphy pen in a flowing font. It clearly wasn't from Bob; he was strictly a Bic man.

There was also a message written on the box: *Handle with care. Your life is in your hands.*

Sylvia stood beside her, and the manager came close, too. Ruby carefully opened the lid. All three of them gasped. It was like lifting the roof off a doll's house. A tiny desk, computer, telephone, filing cabinet, even a garbage can.

Ruby reached out a finger. Of course. Paper, white, folded, smoothed. Edges and creases casting shadows to add a third dimension. A woman sat at the desk, a tiny hand holding a minuscule mouse. Ruby carefully laid her finger on the woman's head. It was more substantial than she'd expected. The woman even looked a little like her; the hair was similar.

There were no other figures but there was a row of hooks on a wall that had windows with curved corners. Like the windows of a trailer. Hanging from the hooks was a top hat and coat tails.

"Is it from the guy with the crutches?"

Ruby imagined Bob sitting at the trailer's little table creating this other world. "No way," she said.

"It's real clever," said the manager. "That figure sitting at the desk looks like you."

"I don't get it," Sylvia said.

"My guess," smiled Ruby, "is it's a proposal."

Sylvia clutched Ruby's arm.

"Not that sort of proposal," said Ruby, and Sylvia loosened her grip. "A business proposal."

The manager groaned. "We're going to lose you, aren't we?"

Ruby put the box gently down on the counter. If she was right, she'd accept Marco's proposal on two conditions. First, managing the circus would be her proper job; she'd never fly with Bob again. Second, she was going to take a vacation. She and Emerald were going to explore the Yukon. They wouldn't leave until they'd seen the northern lights.

Silver Salmon

FIONA HOLDS HER BREATH. SHE COUNTS. SHE DOES HER BEST to coat her throat by swallowing saliva. The cough that's rising is as hard as a heartbeat to stop. It explodes, and women in other beds in the hostel dormitory stir, sigh, and shift. She'll have to get up. She's keeping everyone in the room awake, including herself. There's a sofa downstairs, she remembers. She's got to sleep, got to get better because tomorrow she's going to walk on the Mendenhall glacier, drive crampon spikes into ancient ice. A stamp of her foot could have the same effect as a hammer and a chisel; a giant chunk could split off, crash down the valley. At least that's what she imagines. It's probably what all glacier virgins fear. She doesn't credit herself with having original thoughts. Those are far rarer than most people think; the very idea that thoughts are rare is common. Hers are much the same as everyone else's. Except Steve's.

As long as this cold will let her go tomorrow. She might have caught the cold but now it's the cold that's holding her captive. Yet she came on this trip to Alaska to set herself free. She can't believe she's actually here in Juneau. Looking at the city, when she was on a boat trip this afternoon, the buildings didn't seem to have much of a grip on the land; it was as if the mountains could kick them into the sea at any point. Some of the buildings looked as if they were already bobbing in the water: the governor's neat white house, the little onion on top of the Russian church, all the buildings moving away from her as the current of the Gastineau Channel pulled them out to sea.

Another cough detonates and one of the women in the room sighs loudly. Fiona takes this as a prompt; she has to find that sofa. She untwists her feet from the swaddling of her sleeping bag and slides to the floor. The fleece she puts on is quiet but her trousers are noisy so she leaves the dormitory bare-legged, trailing the sleeping-bag behind her like a wedding dress train. She stops on the landing to put on her trousers and scoops the sleeping bag into her arms before going downstairs.

She's halfway down when she registers that there's a light on in the hostel lounge. It's half-past two in the morning. The light must have been left on by mistake. At the bottom of the stairs, she turns into the lounge. There's someone there. A tall man, broad-backed and wearing a red-and-black checked shirt, is standing by the sink filling the kettle.

There's nowhere else to go. She sits on the sofa as quietly as she can. If she closes her eyes perhaps he'll think she's been there all the time and will let her sleep. But he hears the rustle of the sleeping bag as she slides it over her legs.

"Hi there," he says, turning to face her. He's a bit old for a backpacker. Late thirties at least. He's American, as the largeness and checked-shirtedness have already indicated. "Want some tea?" He puts the kettle on the stove and lights it.

Tea at half-past two in the morning. "No, thank you," Fiona says. Her throat is dry, though, from coughing, and it's true that back home in Falkirk it's mid-morning. "Actually," she says. "I will have one if you don't mind, thank you." She hates the way her politeness is so prissy it's verging on rude. She feels like Charlotte in *A Room with a View* or, more specifically, Maggie Smith playing Charlotte in *A Room with a View*.

She's too tired to smile, but she's in America, Have a Nice Day Land, so she will try. "I'm sorry," she says, not entirely sure what for. "I'm not feeling too good. I've got a cold. I was coughing so much I had to get up before someone in the dorm decided to throw me out the window." She coughs now as if to prove she's telling the truth, as if she doesn't want him to think she's here for any other reason.

The man chuckles and goes to the fridge. He walks with his feet turned a little inward like the bear she saw on Admiralty Island yesterday. He's baggy like a bear, too, and fleshy, not tight and lean like Steve. He walks lightly, though, for such a large man, as he crosses from carpet to lino. Fiona likes this open-plan space, the kitchen and living room area combined, the absence of doors and the walls pushed wide. It's not a big hostel, she thinks, but she can't be sure because she's never stayed in a hostel before. Never been to America before. Never travelled alone before.

"Here," he hands her a glass of water. "This might help. My name's Ray."

"Thank you. That's very kind. My name's Fiona."

"I don't usually lurk in hostel kitchens in the middle of the night," Ray says. "But I'm leaving for my flight in an hour or so and it wasn't worth going to bed. I'm not a great sleeper."

She likes the way the soft grey cotton t-shirt he's wearing under his checked shirt rests against his tanned neck. She pulls her sleeping-bag up to her chin. Ray takes two mugs from a shelf. She's waiting for the accent question.

"You're Scottish, am I right?" Ray leans against the sink. "I love your accent."

Fiona nods. She's only been here a few days but she knows he will tell her what percentage of the blood pumping through his veins is Scottish. Or Irish or Welsh or English. She's actually half-English but she never has any urge to provide strangers with that information.

"I'm an eighth Scottish," he says, "but you must get sick of Americans going on about that. Trouble is, the soil covering our roots is so thin. Anyways, what brought you to Alaska?"

She won't tell him she came because she loves the word Alaska because it feels like a palindrome even though it isn't and makes her think of mountains perfectly reflected in glassy water.

"I've always wanted to come here. Silly really. Clichéd."

"Alaska's that kind of place," Ray says. "Reels folk in like a humongous fishing rod. And once you've come here, you turn into a silver salmon and can't stop coming back. I'm from Texas, that's where I'm flying to. Alaska's even bigger than Texas and that's saying something. My business is there but I'm working on transferring it here. All these flights are getting expensive so I might as well live here." Behind him the kettle is whistling and he twists to take it off the stove.

"What sort of business are you in?"

"Motels." When Ray says this he puts emphasis on the first syllable, as Fiona would if she were saying Motown. He puts the kettle down and turns back to her, as if conversation is more important than tea. "Should be in one now, I guess, but motels are lonely when you're on your own. You must be wondering how I can bring a motel business here when none of the roads go anywhere."

The only thing Fiona is wondering is why he can't make tea and talk at the same time.

"See, I'm going to be buying guesthouses, inns. Maybe even a hostel like this. Not big hotels. I don't think humans are designed to sleep in buildings full of other people they'll never see, let alone talk to. Guess I've got a thing about shelter. Providing roofs over people's heads. It would have been cool to have been a carpenter."

He's quiet while he makes the tea. Fiona wonders if it's because he's concentrating or because he finds her lack of response rude. Right now, she doesn't care. She wants him to go away and let her fall asleep. She likes the idea of falling into sleep. It reminds her of when she was a little girl and swung on a rope out over Lake of Menteith. When she let go, she was expecting the water to be freezing but it was warm because of the heat wave. She could have stayed in forever.

She closes her eyes for a moment and when she opens them again, there's a mug of tea on the coffee table next to her and Ray is sitting at the table in the kitchen end of the room, flicking through a copy of *National Geographic*.

"Thanks," she says, "for the tea."

"You're welcome," Ray smiles. "I didn't want to wake you."

The tea, she finds, is oil for her smile. "This is perfect."

"I'd love to see Scotland," Ray says. "The Cuillin Ridge on the Isle of Skye. That's what I want to see. You live anywhere near that?"

Fiona laughs. "Not by Scottish standards. I live in Falkirk. Quite near Edinburgh," she adds, to help him a little.

"Right. The Royal Mile. The castle. Calton Hill. Holyrood Palace. The parliament," he reels off. "You see? I've done my homework." He pauses. "Aren't we both lucky, to live in such awesome places? I already count myself as Alaskan though I won't be an official resident for another month." He pauses again and they both take a sip of tea. "To tell the truth," he says, not that she asked for it, "there's another reason I'm making the move up here."

Of course there is. People don't come to the end of the world just for the view. "Oh?"

"I'm getting divorced."

This is more interesting than motels and the Royal Mile and possibly more dangerous but the age gap between them is surely way too wide for either of them to be able to jump across.

"How long were you married?"

"Seven years. I say that's the reason I'm moving here but truth is it's the other way round. It's because I want to live here that I'm getting divorced. Pammy, you see, she's Texan through and through. Hates Alaska. Too cold. Too many trees. She can't breathe here. Literally. Gets nosebleeds. Latitude sickness she calls it."

"Sounds familiar." Fiona puts her mug down on the coffee table. "I tried to get my boyfriend to come here with me but he's only interested in sun, sand, and nightlife holidays."

"So you came on your own and left him at home. Good for you," Ray says.

"Well, I didn't just leave him at home. I left him for good."

Ray looks impressed. "So we're kindred spirits, then."

Fiona smiles, although it is largely to herself. Ray is the first person to say anything encouraging about her leaving Steve. Her parents, her friends all tried to talk her out of it. "We split up over where to live, too. Though on a smaller scale. He wanted me to move in with him but I realized I wanted to carry on living with my parents. Then I realized my parents wanted me to move in with him, too."

She stops talking and blushes. No one else knows her parents don't want her to live with them any more, possibly not even her parents.

Ray is silent. He sips his tea, then says, "At least you're still in touch with your folks."

She's disappointed he doesn't say more. She's becoming addicted to North American openness.

After another sip of tea, he looks at his watch and sighs. "I gotta catch that plane."

He pushes the mug away from him, reaches into the pocket of the jacket hanging on the back of his chair and takes out a pen. He starts to write on a page of the *National Geographic* and, when he's finished, carefully tears the page out. A quick rip would have been better. The tear is too noisy for nearly three o'clock in the morning. Fiona imagines the woman upstairs repeating her laboured sigh.

Ray gets up, walks over to her and hands her the page. Across an advert for an expensive watch he's written his name, address, telephone number, email. His writing is neat. He doesn't ask her to give him her contact details.

"I'll give you a job," he says, "if you want. Here in Juneau."

"You don't even know what I do." Fiona starts to laugh, but that makes her cough and she has to drink the last of her tea to soothe her throat. And buy herself time.

"OK. What do you do?"

"Housing association. That's social housing, for people who can't afford their own homes."

"So we're both in the shelter business." He's grinning. "When can you start?"

"I don't think it's that easy," Fiona says. "Don't I need a green card or something?"

"There are ways around that."

She raises her eyebrows.

"Legal ways," he says. Maybe he's closer to his mid-thirties. "Romantic ways," he adds.

Fiona doesn't know whether it's her chafed nose, bloodshot eyes or the way she coughs that has made her so irresistible. He must be mad.

"I'm serious."

"Maybe you'd better go and catch your plane."

SHE STAYS WHERE SHE IS, listening to him drive away in his hire car. When all she can hear is her own snotty inhalations she lies back but quickly sits up again. She has an email to write. The hostel's small computer room is across the hall. She wears her sleeping bag like a waterlogged shawl and sits in front of the monitor.

Dear Steve, she types. She tells him she doesn't love him any more and that she is splitting up with him. It is over. She is very blunt. She knows how easily emails can be misinterpreted and wants to leave no room for ambiguity. She doesn't even say she's sorry.

She presses send and looks at her cowardly fingers. She touches her throat, the ribs of her trachea, and knows her voice is spineless. She should have told him before she left. Even a phone call would have been better than an email. But it seems she has had to come all the way here in order to send a message back. It's the only way to make sure he's really listening. It's unexpected but her cowardice has made her feel braver.

She looks at Ray's magazine page.

She can imagine how it could be, how she could become American and get into the accommodation business and walk down sidewalks and go to restaurants and sleep in the same bed as Ray. It can't happen because Alaska isn't a real place, only a destination to visit, not even a palindrome. She will go home and move out of her parents' house into a place of her own, just her. She's twenty-three. It's time.

ON THE AFTERNOON of the next day, Fiona is standing in a cave made of ice. She waits until she's alone, then stamps in her crampons and tips her head back. The guide said the cave is called the Cathedral. Above her, glistening turquoise, the roof could be one metre away or ten. She can't tell because she's never seen light this way before. She wants to whoop, be American for a moment, and so she does. The ice echo makes her voice sound vast. Outside the cave, on the surface of the glacier, she hears the people in her group laugh and she can tell they're wishing they'd thought of whooping, too.

Magnetic North

HE'S FLYING OVER POLAR BEARS. THEIR HEFTY, SHAGGY SHAPES merge with snow shadows, giving the illusion, sometimes, they're not there. The ridges of the Beaufort Sea could be a mountain range, could be a cracked puddle. All scale is gone. To be in a helicopter looking down on air and ice and water. Already, taking this job is worth it.

This surveying has to be done, data need to be collected before a decision can be made. He's part of it; he should be chuffed. His mother should be chuffed, too, on his behalf. If she understood what he does. He's given up trying to explain why he's always in places he has to fly to, how terrain is his open plan office. He's given up trying to understand why at the age of twenty-four he still needs his mother to understand what he does.

But the bears. A mother and two cubs. Not that he knows much about polar bears, or porcupine caribou, or the other two hundred or so species of birds and mammals whose territory this is. And of course it's human territory, too: the Gwich'in who don't want the caribou chased away because they rely on them for subsistence, though that's hard to believe in this day and age, even up here. And the Inuvialuit, or is it the Vuntut Gwitchin, who he's heard people at the camp talk of, how they should be happy the scientists are here because there could be lots of money in it for them. Dominic doesn't know who really owns this land, whose permission they need to be here, but the important thing is to gather the data so that decisions can be made.

They don't have to swing so far out over the Beaufort but the pilot is even more proud of this seascape than he is of his shiny red helicopter and, anyway, it's useful to get an overview; maps are never detailed or accurate enough, especially not here. There's a hundred-mile tundra plain ahead of them now, tussocked wetlands threaded by a braided river. They're looking out for low bulges, which might mean a salt dome, which might mean a natural oil trap.

This is just a reconnaissance; tomorrow the helicopter will land and they'll start with the magnetometer, find which subterranean rocks have the least magnetism and therefore most attraction for oil prospectors. Perhaps when they return to camp the landslide on the road will have been cleared and they can at last mount the vibrator on the truck and start thumping sound waves down into the rock. That's what he loves most. Out in the field, crouching with a laptop. Where nature and technology prove to be compatible lovers. It makes him feel almost voyeuristic.

THERE'S A LETTER FOR HIM, back at the camp.

"Computers haven't made it to Scotland, then," says the administrator, passing the letter to him. It's his mother's handwriting.

The red and blue blocks along its edges look quaint. They also look time-consuming, as if someone has painted each one by hand.

It was mailed nearly three weeks ago, if he's reading the faint Aberdeen postmark right. It took that long to get here because where he is now doesn't have an address. Main office has sent it on. She's got email, a phone. Why a letter?

Dear Dominic, I've got breast cancer. This is what the letter is saying, except she takes two pages to say it. More than she's ever said to him before in one go. She's right. Email and phone aren't right for this but he's going to have to ring her. If he writes back she won't get it for days. If he calls he'll need to have words to say. He'll write some down first, a script to read over the phone.

If he could only rehearse with someone, imagine out loud how the conversation might go. It's over two years since he had a girlfriend. People, even his mother, have told him he's good-looking and he can see that his features are regular enough and his eyes are blue enough and his hair is dark enough but what he needs is to be good-talking enough. He needs to have something to say to the same person every day for the rest of his life.

"Mum," he says when she picks up the phone. He's probably woken her. It's eleven o'clock in Aberdeen and she's an early-to-bed, early-to-rise type. "I got your letter." It's a start. He has to say more so it's not a finish, too. Everything he wrote down looks stupid now. "I'm so sorry," he says. "How are you feeling?"

He's not surprised she doesn't bother answering his asinine question.

"I'm booked in to have the operation next Tuesday," she says.

"Tuesday." He thinks. "How long have you known?"

"I wasn't going to bother you. But then, I thought, what if I die during the operation?"

His mother is forty-four. Had him young. That doesn't mean she has to do everything young, including dying.

"You'll be fine," Dominic says. "It's only a lumpectomy, right, not a mastectomy. You'll be fine. This'll take care of it." There's no answer.

"Tell you what," he adds. "I'll come back." He's way off his script.

"But it's only a lumpectomy," she parrots. "I'll be fine."

"That's not what I meant."

"So you don't think I'll be fine?"

"Jesus, Mum. Stop it."

"What is it you're doing there exactly?" So she's forgotten again or maybe, maybe she wants the distraction. Perhaps she's not as tough as she sounds, and like a child she's asking for a story to be read over and over again. Or she wants the comfort of his voice, any voice. Maybe the radio would do just as well.

"Oil exploration. Northern Yukon."

"I thought it was gold in the Yukon, not oil."

"All I'm doing is gathering data. If there's evidence it's here it won't be up to us, it'll be up to the government, the aboriginals, to decide whether or not to grant mineral leases."

"You mean let companies drill."

"Yes."

"Bugger up all that wilderness."

How does she know it's wilderness? She's all hearsay, never hard evidence.

"I'm just one of the scientists," he says. "Gathering data. It's important we know whether oil's there or not."

"Is it?" his mother says softly, so softly it's scarcely a question and it's easy to ignore it.

FLYING ACROSS THE ATLANTIC, Dominic is hoping his mother's not going to give him a hard time about his job. Since when did she start caring so much about the environment? She doesn't realize that geophysicists like him only have a ten per cent success rate for finding oil reserves, and only a two per cent chance that the reserves they find contain what's termed commercially useful amounts. Why go to all the trouble, then, she'd probably say in that new quiet voice of hers.

Best not to get into it. Best not to talk about percentages and success rates.

He imagines the rest of his team right now, out on the tundra getting the vibrator going, pictures sound waves bouncing off rocks underground, each pulse recorded on the seismo-graph, translated into computer language, humans all trusting each translation is precise, not a game of Chinese whispers.

His mother has already gone to the hospital when he ar-rives. The doctors thought it would be a good idea, she tells him when he finds her in her private room and kisses her cheek. What does that mean?

And where are her friends, he wonders. Vanessa. Moira. "You have told them, surely?"

"I didn't want any fuss," she says.

He's never seen her looking so tired.

"It's so, well, personal. I wanted family." She says it as a sigh, as if she's wishing for snow on the equator, or everlasting life. What she really means is she wants her dead husband to be there.

"They're your best friends. They care about you, for God's sake. It's not as if you have an awful lot of family." She might have cancer but that doesn't mean he's not allowed to get angry. "There's only your sister and you've never been best buddies. Plus she's in Australia and broke no doubt. There's that small detail. Have you told her?"

His mother shakes her head.

"So you're stuck with me."

"Why come if you didn't want to?" she asks.

"Why d'you twist it round all the time?"

"You're just like your father, you know that? Even when you're with me you don't really want to be. Except he only ever went as far as the garden. You always did have to go to ex-tremes. The Yukon for Christ's sake."

He sits down on a chair by her bed. He'll try. "It's not you," he says. "It's here."

She looks around, lifts her hands as if to take any explana-tion he might be offering.

"Not the hospital," he says. "This country."

She drops her hands back on the bed.

"Every inch has been trampled down," he says, "with a foot or a wheel or, I don't know, a metal detector. I just can't be here, not all the time. The places I'll be able to see, if I'm lucky. If I do a good job. Places hardly anyone gets to see."

"You can't always be the guest. Sometimes you have to be the host."

He wants her to explain what she means but she's closed her eyes and he hasn't the heart to make her open them again.

WHILE HE'S WAITING for her to come out of the operation he surfs the web in an internet café. At first, there is more about support groups than scientific detail. But then he's staring at a cross-section of a breast: ducts, lobules, nipple, and cauliflowers of fat. He's a geophysicist; he can do cross-sections. His mother's breasts — not that he wants to be thinking about them — are small. Once they have removed the lump and some surrounding tissue, there won't be much left. The scalpel will probably be heated to minimize bleeding and the blade might be curved so it makes an incision, like a smile or a frown that follows the natural shape of the breast. This enables it to heal better. The stitches will probably be the type that dissolve.

HE SITS BESIDE HER BED. He's reading a journal he brought with him when he realizes he's missed the moment. Her eyes are already open and she's looking at him.

"Thank you," she says, "for coming." She's crying, trying to get her hand out from under the covers. He hasn't seen her cry since his father died. He gives her his fingers and she clutches them.

"Will you take me?"

"Take you where? Home? No way. Not yet."

"No," she shakes her head. "Take me to the Yukon."

IT'S WEEKS, OF COURSE, before she can manage it. It takes quite
a bit of managing for him, too. Camps don't have open days;
mothers aren't generally allowed to visit geophysicists' camps
or go up in contract helicopters. Yet what, Dominic says to his
boss, if the cancer returns? She's on Tamoxifen but there's no
knowing. His boss knows. His mother died of breast cancer, he
says. He has four grown-up children, two girls, two boys, and
one of his sons has got breast cancer now.

DOMINIC MEETS HER at Whitehorse airport. He can't remember ever having seen her outside Aberdeen before. Her back-
drop is grey granite that glitters in the rain, not mountain
snow that glitters in the sun. She never took him to London
or even Edinburgh. That was his father. Aberdeen is big —
has everything from shops to beaches — but not so big you
shouldn't leave it sometimes. Maybe it's partly his fault for going to university in Aberdeen, because he thought he ought to
be near his widowed mother.

They fly to Dawson City where they stand on the gravel
runway and he helps her into a tiny plane.

"It's fantastic," she laughs after they've taken off and he's
pointing out Tombstone Mountain. "How much do these
things cost? I want one."

"The mountains or the plane?" he says.

She laughs too much. It wasn't that funny.

THEY LAND ON AN AIRSTRIP that looks too short and she stays
in her seat for as long as she can, like a child who doesn't want
to get off a fairground ride. But then she's giggling with the pilot as if flirting will persuade him to take her up again. He has
a nasty thought. Maybe, because of the operation, she thinks
she has to work harder now at being female.

The helicopter is waiting for them and they crouch and
climb into it. The same pilot swings them out over the Beaufort Sea, but there are no polar bears this time.

"That's Alaska," shouts Dominic, gesturing at a haze of endless blue to the west.

Down on the ground, balanced on a tundra mattress, she's chatting to his research colleagues as if she's been travelling to places like this all her life. Dominic suggests they walk a hundred metres or so to a braid of river. Halfway there, his mother stops at the edge of a patch of berries. She bends down and cups a small orange fruit like an unripe raspberry in her hand. "We can't tread on a wee thing like that."

"Cloudberries," Dominic says. "The grizzlies love them. The Inuit make a kind of ice cream with them, beat up the berries, mix them up with seal oil, chewed caribou tallow. And they use the leaves as a kind of tea. In Alaska, I think, they call them salmon berries because they look like salmon eggs."

"You're quite the encyclopaedia." She says it with Aberdeen glitter in her eye.

Dominic laughs. "Not really. There are a few books at the camp that people have left behind."

He has an urge to tell her more, a little boy trying to impress his mother. How the Inuit have different names for cloudberries as they go through each stage. *Aqpiqutit* before the berry forms. *Aqpiksait* during spring, before they turn red. *Aqpit* in summer. He can't tell her these words because, although he can see them in his mind, and can even spell them, he doesn't know how to say them.

"This, believe it or not, is a full-grown willow tree." He bends down beside his mother and touches a tiny leaf with one finger. "They can't grow high like trees down south because of the permafrost. A few inches under our feet the ground is permanently frozen. It's like a natural bonsai."

Smiling, his mother stands up and puts her hands on her hips. "Your father would have adored it here. I'd never have got him away from somewhere like this. He should have been some kind of researcher like you. A botanist maybe. He was always in the bloody garden, after all." She pauses. She's staring northward, as if she's trying to see where the river is going. "He'd be so glad you know about these things. Maybe if he'd had a job like this, a job he loved, he wouldn't have had his heart attack so young."

"Heart attacks are physiological, genetic," Dominic says, still crouched. "Diet and exercise make the difference, not how much you like your job."

She looks down at him and he can't tell if it's with pity or envy.

"Actually" — Dominic stops. He nips off a cloudberry, eats it, and plucks off several more. "Here." He stands up and pours a handful into his mother's palm. "Good for you. Antioxidants, I think."

His mother puts one in her mouth and winces.

"You get used to the tartness."

"What were you going to say?" she asks him.

He takes a couple of berries back from her, puts them in his mouth and talks as he eats. "I was trying to keep it separate. You know, the science and the morals. But I think there are things we don't need to know. You can't use science to justify wrong decisions. If drilling goes ahead here it will ruin this place. You said it yourself."

"Did I?"

"Yes, on the phone, back when I got your letter. And what about the people whose land this really is? What if they don't get to have their say?"

"You think you're going to resign."

"I don't think it. I'm going to."

"No, you're not."

"Christ, Mum, have some faith in me."

"It's not about you." She bends to pick more berries. "It's the way things are. You'll never find any job, anything at all, where you don't have to make some sort of compromise, where there won't be some kind of moral dilemma."

He stops watching her head, the wind waving her hair about. The hair she may lose if the cancer hasn't been cut out. She's so sure of herself. How can anyone be sure about anything, if you can have something inside you that's killing you and not even know?

"I did some reading, too, before I came," she says, standing again. She puts a berry in her mouth. "God knows I didn't have anything else to do. You won't agree with this, being a scientist, but I was reading about how the Inuit, the people you were talking about, how they believe that even inanimate objects have a spirit. Every plant we're standing on, every pebble in that river."

They both look over at the shining curve of water and start walking toward it at the same time.

"I think that when we love a place," Dominic's mother continues as they walk, "bits of us enter it and get all mixed in with the atoms and what not. Maybe that's where the spirit in these berries and stones and bonsai willows really comes from. From the people who love it here."

When they reach the river, she turns to look at him. "I think that's what's happened to you. You're part of this place now. You can resign if you want, it's up to you, but you'll never actually leave here, not completely."

She's not looking at him; she's looking at the water.

Dominic stretches both of his arms up toward the sky. "I submit," he says. He says it again, loudly. He looks at his mother's face and she's smiling.

He lowers his arms and picks up a small stone. He tries not to note that it's argillite, which can easily be a billion years old, only that its roughness feels good in his palm and the dark grey is flecked with white like starlight. He hands it to his mother. "Take this," he says. "Take this home with you so that you'll always have a part of me."

Carbonated

Walk in a circle to keep warm. Tread down the steps. Walk back up the ramp. Do this ten times. Only then look at your watch and worry why Tim isn't here yet.

On the third circuit, Abby catches the eye of the Filipina cleaner on the egg-yolk warm side of the locked glass door. The cleaner looks away; it's not her job to deal with loiterers. The library closed one hour and — Abby checks her watch and will now have to start the circuits from scratch again if she's going to follow her rules — eleven minutes ago.

Don't put an ungloved hand on the metal railing; You'll lose core heat. The blood in your fingers that got nice and warm travelling round your guts will cool and flow right back to your heart. Don't take your hands out of your pockets. Pull your thin scarf over your head; it doesn't matter what you look like.

He went to see a man about a job.

She doesn't even know where except it's a village to the north and she thought they were already north. Hour and a half north, the man on the phone told Tim. She wanted to know how many miles that was, or kilometres, but Tim had hung up and when she asked him again he shrugged and told her she could look it up in the library while she was waiting for him. Abby had hated him then. She knew it was best to say nothing. She was familiar with such rage from period days, how it turned her mouth into a blowtorch.

She has no idea what temperature it is in centigrade, Celsius, or Fahrenheit. Except it's cold, getting colder. A man walks by on the pavement — sidewalk — in front of the library. She tries to look as if she and the temperature are good friends. She uncurls her fingers and lifts her hands out of her pockets. Not for long.

In London, you learn never to look vulnerable out of doors, on the tube, walking home along Uxbridge Road after dark. In London, the weather is an irritation, never a threat; an amorous drunk after a night at his local, not a rapist.

A dark car is coming along the street. It carries on past the entrance to the library car park — parking lot. Tim is a good driver. Perhaps he has stopped to help someone who has broken down. Perhaps he has broken down himself; they have had to trust the man they paid to check the car was safe, because there's no such thing as an MOT certificate in this place.

Breathe from your navel. Don't suffocate the panic, it will only have to fight its way out. The moon. Stare at it. Look for the Sea of Tranquillity.

She's shivering. The tip of her nose is numb. It's not cold enough to get frostbite, surely, but if she's out here long enough, could it happen? Her toes. She wiggles them and they hurt. She'll do more circuits. The other way round: down the ramp, then up the steps. When the librarian locked the door, the moon was to the left of the aspens. Now it's an x-ray making skeletons of them. Before they came, Abby's sister emailed them a link to a photograph showing Earth at night. This place they have come to was one of the darkest of all. Darker than the Amazon.

You could say, as Mum did, that cities at night are pretty, like Christmas. So are silvery, shivery aspens until you find out that the sheen on every leaf is painted by moth larvae so tiny that four of them would fit on a mosquito's back (she can see them, a saddle each and the front one holding the reins) and nobody knows yet if the trees will survive this occupation.

Usually, Abby likes night. When she sits on the deck of the cabin they are renting, she at first sees nothing. Other senses are quicker; she feels a breeze on her face and hears it snag and tear on branches, like the clothes of someone running through the woods. She sniffs green-tea earth and hears the waves on the lake throw themselves at the shore. Then at last she sees watery washes of clouds above a scratchy spruce horizon.

THE FIRST NIGHT SHE DID THIS, Tim came out, the screen door slamming behind him.

What on earth are you doing? You must be mad. It's freezing out here.

Abby could hear, almost see, the noise of him ripple across the lake. She tried to stay out after he'd gone back in but it didn't work; her senses had switched off. The next night, though, it worked. That time, Tim didn't come out to see what she was doing. She wished he had; she loves the sound of the screen door slamming.

IT's ALMOST HALF-PAST TEN; he said he'd be here by seven or so. She doesn't want to know what that means. She doesn't have anyone to ring. They may never have anyone here they know well enough to call. She must keep moving.

She trips on the bottom step, flings her hands out to break her fall. Her palms smash into concrete. They're not cut but they sting. A lot. She needs to be indoors; she doesn't know what time pubs close here or where one is. They haven't been to a bar yet. You can't spend money drinking when you've nothing coming in to wash it down. At least Tim can't. Joblessness is an injury. Supermarket shopping inflicts pain. Tim wouldn't even let her buy a bag of crisps or any chocolate. He snatched them from the trolley and put them back on the shelves as if she were a child. The blowtorch was lit and she pressed her lips together, swallowing fire.

Luxuries, he said. We can buy luxuries again when we've found jobs. Not until.

For Christ's sake, we're not penniless, Abby said, her mouth burning. We have savings.

We won't if we keep spending it all, Tim said.

She could leave a note on the door and look for a hotel. She has a plaster — a Band Aid — in her bag, she could use it to attach a piece of paper, a page from her CV — her resumé — if she can't find anything else.

What if the cleaner, or anyone, removes the note? He won't know how to find her. They have forgotten how to exist apart.

When he left her on Second Avenue that morning, it was the first time they had separated since they arrived. Watching the car move away, it looked tiny; she held her finger and thumb up and it fitted easily inside.

She had at least five hours to herself. Nobody knew where she was inside this town and if she left it, no one would know where she went or why. She'd felt excitement rise. She had to breathe, raise her ribs, to make room for this sudden bubbling under her sternum, like the froth from a carbonated drink that might or might not hiss over the rim. She'd had this fizzy feeling before, when the plane lifted them from England. It was the sensation of possibility.

She found a bookshop and bought a novel, with cash so there wouldn't be a record of the purchase on their bank statement. The bubbling feeling remained inside her lungs. At a café, she ordered a latté and muffin. As she read, the fizz bubbled between her lips and made them tickle and smile; she had to time her sips of latté carefully.

When she left the café she sniffed deeply to take as many coffee molecules with her as she could. Standing on the sidewalk, she raised and turned her face, a sunflower, to the sun. When she opened her eyes the tops of the mountains were so snow-bright she couldn't look at them.

SHE STOPS IN THE LIGHT of the library door and wraps her scarf more tightly round her head to shield her ears. The bubbles popped, the fizz flattened before the library closed, before she had to go outside and wait here in the cold. Now, it seems that a chemical reaction has occurred and carbonation has calcified into stones that have dropped to the bottom of each lung. She cannot breathe enough air; the stones have reduced her lung capacity and are in danger of blocking her trachea.

It wasn't because she was away from Tim; it was because she was on her own. The difference is everything. It came to her by accident, she didn't seek it.

She doesn't have the phone number of the man he was meeting, only his first name, Mike. She can't get back to the cabin she and Tim are renting because it is more than thirty miles away and there is no public transport. That's the point of the wilderness.

A note on the door and an expensive taxi to the phoneless cabin.

Or the police. Who will laugh at her, drive her home, tell her off for wasting their time but still come in for a cup of tea. She is thinking of police in 1950s England who do not exist anywhere any more. She has never met a Mountie. Nor does she much want to now.

DRIVING NORTH TO THIS PLACE a week ago, they laughed a lot. The horizontal snowflakes, they said, were stars and they were travelling at warp speed through space. They had expected, said Tim, to drive out of summer but they hadn't expected to miss the turning to autumn and find themselves in winter.

No wonder we missed it, Abby said. We're looking for a

sign for autumn when we should be looking for a sign for fall. We've got to learn the local lingo.

AFTER ATTACHING A NOTE to the door with the Band Aid, Abby follows the map to find the RCMP building. She walks as slowly as she can even though she knows her vulnerability rating is consequently too high, off the scale each time she takes the map out of her pocket. She looks for moving cars but there are few now. Everyone is already where they want to be.

The police, Mounties, don't laugh at her. They hand her milkless tea and ask her why she isn't dressed properly.

I left my gloves, Abby says, in the car. Which is true, except they are taper-fingered city gloves.

Along with your toque and boots, says one officer whose eyes know her nod is really a shake.

They take her to a motel in a police car even though it's only three blocks away. If he is dead she will go home. Home, home. If he is missing she will ask Mum for money. If he is okay she will leave him. She wants the fizz back, the stones gone.

The phone rings at four in the morning and she runs to the lobby with her coat over her shoulders and bare feet in her shoes. There is no time for socks.

Everyone here knows how big moose are. But caribou are big, too, especially the males, the bulls, the RCMP officer calls them. When a hefty-antlered bull caribou hits a vehicle, the animal and the driver are lucky if they survive. It is rare that both do.

TIM IS LYING ON HIS BACK on the bed after she has collected him from the hospital and she is running him a bath. She won't add any cold water unless she has to. That no bones are snapped when the car is a write-off is unbelievable. But capillaries are crushed, muscle tissue is torn, and skin is split.

Antlers, he murmurs. I saw antlers looming out of the snow. Warp speed?

She watches but he doesn't smile.

Caribou are the same as reindeer, Abby says.

No Christmas presents for me then. Just as well because the car and this motel have wiped us out.

A joke, of sorts. So he is all right even if he has no vigour for a smile.

As she drives them back to the cabin in a rental car, Tim dozes and winces and she tries not to see all the dark spaces between all the trees and there are so many trees. Even though she can feel the wind pushing at the car, the lake, when they reach it, looks glutinous, like a tray of fudge left to set. She's heard that people light fires on the ice once it's thickened but she won't believe it unless she sees it.

Now that she knows what she is going to do, the stones have gone.

She follows Tim into the cabin and watches as he tries to set the cold wood stove. He can lift a sheet of newspaper but can't screw it up. He can lift sticks of kindling one by one and drop them inside the stove but she can see he won't be able to strike a match. He doesn't have the strength.

I have a question, she says, and you have to answer it without asking me what my answer is.

He turns, carefully, to look at her. I don't get it, he says, but go on then.

She goes over to the stove, takes out the kindling he's put inside and starts to set the fire again.

If you could fly home tomorrow, she says, rolling a sheet of newspaper into a belt, would you go? Home to England, I mean.

He looks at her but she won't look at him. She ties a knot in the belt, something he taught her to do.

Okay, Tim says. I'll give you an answer. I would do whatever you did. No, let me change that. I will do whatever you do.

That's not what I asked, she says, adding more newspaper.

Maybe not, but that's my answer.

Abby places kindling on top of the newspaper. Because of his answer, she has changed her mind. Yet the stones have not come back. She picks up the box of matches.

We're going to Mark's Work Wearhouse tomorrow, she tells him. We're going to buy proper winter gear. Sorel boots. Down jackets.

Tim doesn't say anything. She doesn't look at him.

By the way, she adds as she strikes a match, you didn't tell me how the job interview went.

Never even found him, Tim says. His directions were crap. No one knew who I was talking about. Complete waste of time.

The Ladies of Marsh Lake

NICOLA LEANS ON HER POLES TO STEADY HERSELF. SHE'S USED to being good at sports, used to people wanting her on their team, to being the chooser of teams. Yet she finds cross-country skiing confusing. How is it possible to push, slide, and balance all in one movement?

"Imagine you're creeping up on someone from behind," says Monique, who's standing easily on her skis a few feet away, her poles poking air as she adjusts her hat. "that's the motion you're aiming for."

Nicola crouches a little, tips her shoulders forward.

"Your ass," Monique says, "don't stick it out. You look as if you're about to pee."

Nicola doesn't know if she likes Monique.

There's a stunning view here. Nicola straightens up and inhales, chilled air yanking her nose hairs. The lake down the hill is white. The mountains on the other side of the lake are white. Only the blue sky is snowless. The dark spruces all around them are balancing blobs of Mr. Whippy ice cream on their branches.

The Yukon is beautiful, Nicola can see that. Except she's used to wanting to live in the beautiful places she visits and she's not sure she could live here. She's not competent enough, not like Monique and her posse of female friends who build houses in the summer, shoot moose in the autumn, and change their own car tyres each winter.

"You're doing great," Monique says.

Nicola wrinkles her nose.

"You're used to being able to do everything right first time, aren't you."

"If only," Nicola says. She's thinking of Ben.

"Here," Monique says, "nature's in control. That sounds sappy but it's true. Once you get that, you'll do fine."

YESTERDAY, NICOLA HADN'T KNOWN a soul in the whole Yukon. She'd been in a café on Main Street in Whitehorse staring up at the list of lattes and espressos when Monique, behind her in the queue, told her to try a matcha. Nicola's English accent had piqued Monique's interest and they'd sat at a table together. Within twenty minutes Nicola was invited to come stay with Monique south of town in Marsh Lake. It is what Nicola has been looking for, a tranquil place where no one knows her, a remote place where she can send the occasional postcard to her parents and friends and they'll assume she isn't ringing or emailing because there's no telephone or internet service here. After all, the Yukon is in the middle of nowhere.

When Monique turned off the highway and down the drive to her house, the scene was as Canadian as maple syrup: log house, snow, forest, frozen lake. And two impossibly neat stacks of wood, each longer than Monique's truck and easily as tall. One stack was made up of whole logs, all cut to the same length. The stack next to it, closer to the house, contained only split logs. Their triangular ends made a pretty pattern.

"Those piles are so neat. How do you do that?" said Nicola as Monique parked the truck in front of the house.

"We work together. Me, Wendy, and Ariel." Monique switched off the ignition and stayed sitting behind the wheel. "Wendy and Ariel have lots either side of mine. We're like a little commune." She smiled. "We go into the bush off the highway every summer. Spend all day felling dead spruce, limbing them and cutting them into eighteen-inch lengths with a chainsaw. Monique opened the truck door and stepped down to the snow. "We work until we each have five cords. Often takes a couple of weeks."

"Cords?" said Nicola, clambering out of the truck without any of Monique's grace.

"Four by four by eight foot."

"And that's to heat your house?"

"Yup. And we get our water from the lake," said Monique, leading Nicola down the side of the house instead of to the front door. "Pump it up winter and summer into big tanks in our basements. We like to live as simply as we can. Meat from hunting. Home-grown veggies in summer. Berry picking in fall. I'll show you my basement. I pickle anything that grows. Tried spruce tips for the first time this year."

"Wow." At home in London — the home she no longer had — all Nicola did was turn up the thermostat for heat, turn on a tap for water, and nip out to Tesco's for ready meals.

"We do have power, though. We're not off the grid."

"You said you have a job in Whitehorse?" said Nicola, noticing skis, a snowmobile, and more wood stored under the house's overhang.

"Yeah. Yukon government. Health and Social."

"Full-time?"

Monique nodded. "It's Saturday today if you're wondering."

"I'm losing track," Nicola said.

Monique pushed the back door open and went in. It wasn't locked.

The journey from Whitehorse took . . . what, an hour? Nicola's commute to work in London on the Tube was shorter than that. Just. How did Monique fit it all in?

Nicola followed Monique wordlessly into the house.

MONIQUE'S HOUSE was as gorgeous on the inside as it was on the outside. The walls were honeyed log and the floor was gleaming wood, too. It wasn't like English houses that had rooms and hallways and doors. It was open plan. The hallway became the kitchen that became the living room that became the balcony looking over the lake.

The room Nicola was staying in had a window seat. That first night she sat there watching the cloudy green shimmer of what she knew were the Northern Lights, even though she'd never seen them before. She watched them silently on her own until Monique called her to come look.

MONIQUE IS TAKING NICOLA to meet her neighbours, Ariel and Wendy. They're trudging through snow along the connecting trails between their houses. The Sorel boots that Monique has lent Nicola are too big. That's why she keeps tripping.

Monique is telling Nicola more about her friends.

"We've all given up on men," Monique says.

"You know about emotional intelligence, right? Let's just say it's not a skill men have developed yet."

They step over a fallen tree, its skinny trunk dense with short scratchy branches. "I'll come back with my saw," Monique mutters.

"More fire wood?"

"Once it's dried out, yeah. So, have you got a partner back home?"

It's the usual question; Nicola is surprised Monique hasn't asked sooner. She shakes her head, even though she's behind Monique. "It depends," she says, "who you ask."

Monique laughs. Nicola laughs too. She's allowed to. Ben isn't here to tell her she laughs when she shouldn't, when things aren't at all funny. She'd thought that had been one of their things — finding humour in the ordinary, the absurd, even the horrific. She even had to stop making jokes about never getting married or having children because Ben didn't think those jokes were funny any more. Not now they were in their thirties for God's sake and you couldn't just carry on making fun of everything. You had to take some things seriously or what was the point? What was the point, Nicola?

"When couples come to the Yukon," Monique tells her, "only one of them usually stays. So you're already one step ahead."

"I'm not staying," Nicola says. "I'm just travelling for a while."

"Right," says Monique.

WENDY AND ARIEL are sitting at Monique's large dining table. Nicola takes a sip of the beer Ariel has handed her and Monique puts a large heavy dish on the table. Thick floury gravy coats the fat chunks of meat.

"Yum," says Wendy, who has blue eyes and smiles a lot as if she's already got the joke. Nicola suspects Wendy is the one who will break the no-men rule first.

"Moose," Monique says, looking at Nicola. "Ever had it? This is the chilli chocolate recipe."

The women whoop.

Nicola shakes her head. "No," she says, "I haven't. The thing is, I'm vegetarian." She has already told Monique this.

"But this is wild meat," Monique says. She spoons a dollop onto Wendy's plate first as if she's giving time for Nicola to think about it.

"Humans are omnivores," Wendy states. "I totally get being opposed to caged meat, hormones and cruelty and sustainability and all that, but this moose died on the land. He was old. The wolves were on to him. There was wolf scat everywhere. A bullet is way quicker. Ever seen a wolf kill?"

"Of course she hasn't," Ariel says. "Even I haven't and I pretty much grew up on the land."

Ariel is aboriginal. They are called First Nation here. Nicola likes that. The people who were here before anyone else. What does that make her? Second Nation, perhaps. The English have a way of getting everywhere. Or Third or Fourth Nation if the Russians or the Scots got here first.

Ariel nods at Nicola. "Wendy is an awesome hunter. She stalks like an animal."

"Like she stalks her ex-husbands," Monique says. They all laugh.

"Killing the weak improves the overall species," Wendy says, and the women laugh louder. "We pay too much attention to individuals rather than the group. This moose was weak." She grins. "This moose wasn't useful any more." Wendy stresses the word moose as if it's a euphemism.

"So, are you trying to tell me this isn't moose?" Nicola says. "It's your ex-husband in this dish?"

Wendy whoops and raises a palm towards Nicola. Nicola catches on and raises her hand to give Wendy a high five.

Monique puts a plate in front of Nicola, smiling. "Try it," she says.

Nicola hasn't eaten meat since she was eighteen. Since she made a pact with Ben and his brown cow-eyes. It's the only pact they have left. It was so easy to leave him to come to Canada, yet breaking their last pact is going to be hard.

"This moose lived as it should," Monique says. "It's probably the best way to die, shot cleanly with one bullet when you're not expecting it. That's how I'd like to go."

"We're doing them a favour," Wendy says.

"When the time comes, will you do the same for each other?" Nicola asks, grinning. She's imagining Wendy aiming a gun at Monique, old and grey, as she bends to pick up a log from the woodpile.

"Sure," Wendy says. "Then, as we've established, we'll eat each other."

"Good idea," Nicola says, keeping it going. "You won't have to worry about buying a burial plot or the cemeteries getting overcrowded."

Ariel is large-eyed, as if the idea of a cemetery being full has never occurred to her. "Is England very crowded?"

"Let's just say I'd call Vancouver a town, not a city."

"You should check out Toronto," Monique says, sitting down.

They each have a plate of moose stew in front of them now.

"What did you say the recipe is?" Nicola asks.

"Chilli and chocolate."

"It's awesome," Ariel says. "It would be brutal not to try it. I know, let's hold hands."

They do.

Ariel closes her eyes. "We are grateful for being here together around Monique's table. We are grateful to the moose who died to give us sustenance. Thank you, moose."

"Thank you, moose," everyone repeats. Only Wendy giggles.

Man, moose, woman. There's no difference. Everyone dies. This moose lived free range, knew death all its life, death coming closer the way that clouds do, not at the end of a life spent pressed against metal bars.

Nicola picks up her fork and pushes it into a chunk of meat. It's soft and looks like tinned dog food. The last animal she ate was a cow, a burger on the high street. Ben had been holding her hand and explaining why this must be her last one ever. She had sipped Coke to cleanse her lips before he would kiss her. She is tired of living by his code. It's time she lived by her own.

She expects to have to chew. There's no need; the meat falls apart on her tongue and it takes no effort to swallow. She can taste the chocolate, and the chilli doesn't burn like she thought it would.

Truck Camper

AMBER THRUST AN ARM OUT, THUMB TAUT AS A GYMNAST, fingers fisted. She dipped her arm as the RV whooshed past, the size of a Greyhound and towing a Tracker. Florida plates. Next, Arizona plates. Even bigger but minus the toy car. The drivers, men, dodged eye contact but the shotgun wives sure didn't, mouths busy over the sight of a girl hitchhiking.

She was getting out of this pit-stop town where the only thing people ever came to see was a load of signs all pointing to other places. People called it the Signpost Forest, but what was the point when you were already inside the largest forest in the universe. Never mind the spruce beetles, the spruce trees themselves were the infestation.

First she'd find a job in Whitehorse, the town that faked being a city. The day she had enough for an air ticket, she'd take off for a real city: Vancouver. Calgary. Edmonton. After that, who knew?

A truck camper was coming toward her. Amber dropped her arm faster than a bird bounced off a windshield. She backed closer to the puny spruces behind her, but the camper stopped anyway.

"Miss the bus?"

Shrug. She wasn't going to tell Betty pie-fingers anything she didn't have to. Betty owned the Milestone Hotel where Amber had worked last summer. Not that she'd ever seen Betty there.

"Heading for Whitehorse?" Betty said.

Nod. Betty had trouble keeping makeup on her face, probably because her constant talking caused too much motion. And the woman didn't so much dye her hair as drown it, jet black this time. No wonder husband Ralph was couch surfing around town again. Meanwhile, people were saying Betty was going everyplace in her camper so that Ralph wouldn't be able to set up home in it. Betty and Ralph's marriage reminded Amber of the time moths got into her mom's closet and chewed bullet holes into one of her coats. Even though her mom didn't like that coat and never wore it, she was still mad.

"Get in then, girl."

Amber had been hoping for an RV, not a runty camper.

"Going on a trip?" Betty said, pulling away.

"Maybe."

Betty shut up but Amber knew she'd throw a bundle of sticks at the nest during the five hours of so-called scenery between them and the city. Curiosity round here was genetic. Not that anything new ever happened; the same events just got circulated like library books. Like Betty always taking Ralph back again.

Four minutes. "Your hair sure looks nice like that, shorter. You don't look so much like your mom any more, though."

Two minutes. "You're graduating next year, aren't you?"

Shrug.

It was Amber's favourite season: the brown phase before the grass recovered from six months of suffocation by snow. Soon as it got itself green, down came the snow again.

"Your dad was the smartest student in his class," Betty said.

Almost a change in subject. "Were you in school with him?" Amber said, staring straight ahead. The hood sucked up pavement like a vacuum cleaner.

Betty showed too much gum when she laughed. "I was his teacher. That's why I'm going to Whitehorse this weekend, to see some of my old teacher friends."

Amber didn't know Betty had been a schoolteacher. She thought she knew everything there was to know about everyone in town.

"I always thought your dad would end up as a big shot down south," Betty said. "But he was just a kid, your age, when your mom got pregnant."

The movie of mom and dad. Just as well no one ever watched the scenes behind closed doors. Mom always had the starring role in those, too.

"Still, he did the right thing by her. Dropped out of high school. Got himself a job. But it's a pity he never graduated."

Amber shrugged. "School's not for everyone."

Betty glanced back at the rear seat where Amber's backpack lay like a dead coyote. "I'm just saying, shame he didn't make more of himself."

Just like mom said to dad every day. But mom said it with whiskey and cigarettes in her voice, not tea and cookies the way Betty did.

"I went to the prairies once," Betty said after a few minutes of peace. "Thought the sky was going to fall in on me. Now I know what all these trees are for. The thing is, there's nothing more important than graduating. I know everyone tells you that, but it's true."

No one at home had ever told Amber that.

The idea of going back to school wasn't the problem; she liked school. What she couldn't face was another year of living with mom hammering dad into the ground like a tent peg. Especially now that mom had broken so many pegs on stony soil she was looking around for softer earth. Amber's best friend Nicole told her that her Mom had been seen with Dan, the auto repair guy, at the Sundog bar. More than once.

"How long you staying in Whitehorse?"

"Not sure."

"Tell you what. See that pen? Write my cell down, 334-4920.

Go on. You can come back with me Sunday. I could use the company. Though that backpack looks like you've got all your worldly possessions with you."

Amber pulled her phone out of her pocket. "I'll put it in here."

"Even better."

Amber slid her phone back into her jeans. At least it would shut Betty up.

"What about a place to stay?"

Amber shrugged. She hadn't got that far in her planning.

"Stay with me at my daughter's. She's got tonnes of room."

"Could do. Thanks." Amber stared up at the sky through the turquoise filter on the windshield. When her eyes came back down, the mountains looked like they had frosting on them. "Can I ask you something, Betty?"

"Absolutely anything."

"Is it possible to change schools? I mean, could someone switch to Whitehorse?"

Betty kept her eyes on the road. "I'm sure that's possible. Why don't you come and meet my teacher friends? We'll ask them."

Manniit

It's her second day here in this place where water, land, and sky merge, but she hasn't met him yet.

She's emailed him regularly over the past few months, imagining winged envelopes of electricity flying over the Clyde, across a curved ocean, above the ice floes. Communication is easy, yet she has no idea how the messages pass from one computer to another or why the words and letters don't get jumbled up. Perhaps emails transmit only because she believes in them. Faith is the transducer.

In his emails, he calls himself Kenu, so Jenny does too.

Really, he has two first names. His mother named him Peter but when he was seventeen he decided that he would be Kenujuak. He knew who he was; evidently his mother, when she first met him, didn't.

But he says — writes — that he understands. He knows how it was then, when there was significance in giving your child a white name. That if thirty thousand people were dissolved into the rest of the world's five or so billion they would be as imperceptible to the taste buds as a teaspoon of sugar in an Olympic-sized swimming pool. And perhaps it was better to get the dissolution over with as quickly as possible.

His mother is different now. She crouches closer to her wide land. Kenu writes to Jenny that he thinks his mother is becoming an *angakok*, a shaman, and that her reincarnation has begun too soon, before her body has died. He isn't sure whether a transmigration has already taken place, or if there are two *inua*, or souls he explains, present. It seems like it; he can see a struggle in the changing rhythm of her muscles. Sometimes, one of her hands is as cold as snow while the other is hotter than the melted wax of the seal-fat candle she lights to read herself to sleep. She marvels at this, reaches out her fingers for her son to feel.

LAST NIGHT, WHEN JENNY RANG Kenu from the research centre and heard his voice for the first time, she was surprised not to recognize it after speaking to him for so many months electronically. She hadn't been expecting him to sound so masculine, or so North American. He had the rise of intonation at the end of his sentences that she's so familiar with from Australian soap operas, and that is apparently as native to this continent, too.

She's due at his studio in less than an hour but she can't leave the research building yet because it's minus twenty-one degrees outside and if she arrives too early she'll freeze. She brought the navy salopettes with her that she went skiing in at school. But every time she goes outside, it's just seconds before the cold starts numbing her thighs. When she first pulled them on over her trousers, hooking the straps over her shoulders, she was simultaneously surprised they still fitted and disappointed they weren't any looser. She's always been big, fleshy as a seal.

IT'S EASY TO FIND HER WAY. He's given her good directions to his studio. She's already familiar with some of the streets from yesterday's explorations to the edges of the town to look for the joins between snow, sea, and sky. As she walks, she folds her street map around the piece of paper she wrote Kenu's directions on and eases them both, crackling, into her pocket. She doesn't want to look like the tourists she sees from time to time.

The town isn't picturesque; there's an igloo-shaped church that she visited yesterday but little else besides scattered, boxy buildings, mostly white but sometimes pale yellow, blue, or red. They look as if they have been erected where they are because that's where the materials happened to have been set down. Apparently each one is built on stilts dug into frozen earth, although she's seen no evidence of this, perhaps because of the snow. When she rakes the snow she's walking on with the toe of her boot the earth is loose underneath; none of the roads is paved here.

She passes a school that looks like an enormous plastic toy brick on which a child has painted geometric lines with a paintbrush. At the corner of the street where she should find Kenu's studio she smiles at the octagonal red stop sign; it's bi-lingual, underneath the English word is one she cannot read, pronounce, or write.

She arrives at Kenu's studio twelve minutes early, so she turns to walk back to the Northern Store to absorb the warmth between the aisles. She went there for the first time yesterday and saw that an apple costs three dollars; she will need to shop carefully here.

She has only taken a few steps when a voice, almost familiar, calls to her. She turns and sees a beautiful face. One she would like to touch with the tips of her fingers and then sculpt, pressing on pellets of soft clay to form those rounded cheekbones, scraping back to create the smiling brow below a short black fringe. But she hasn't played with clay since she was a child.

She follows him back to his studio. His coat is one of those broad, padded jackets that look as if they need to be kept inflated with a bicycle pump. The bottom of it only comes down to hips, revealing the frailty of his pelvis. His trousers are loose and made out of a silky material that looks too thin to keep him warm in this weather. Perhaps to him this isn't such a cold day. It's spring, after all.

As he removes his coat she sees there is a bar of strength in his swimmers' shoulders, hooked through his clavicles and his scapulas. She can see now how he, lean as a wolf, can do it. Hammer and chisel rocks and stones. Strap boulders to his snowmobile and bump across the wiry tundra.

"It's weird to meet you at last," he tells her. She's glad he's said it.

"You're not how I imagined you," she says, then regrets it, for not only is it a cliché but now he'll ask her what she had imagined. Yet he doesn't ask and so she wonders why. She leans against a workbench, squashing her bottom which feels broad in the salopettes. She's too cold to take them off, though.

"Would you rather work while we talk," she says, "while I ask you questions? Do you mind if I watch you work? Is it okay if I record our conversation?"

"Yes to everything," he says. "On one condition?"

"What?"

"That you'll have dinner with me tonight? With me and my mom at home?"

Jenny smiles. "That's difficult," she says. "I'm vegetarian."

Kenu laughs loudly. "You never told me that in your emails. You sure are in the wrong place, you know?" He laughs again.

Jenny knows. Her fellow students at the university have spent the last year reminding her.

"Come anyway," Kenu says. "No problem. Hey, you should take those off, you know." He's nodding at her legs, sounding parental. "Or you'll be cold when you go back out." He pronounces "out" as if it rhymes with "boat." She repeats it inside her head, trying to remember it. Hoping he'll say it again when she's got the recorder running, not that it has anything to do with her research.

"I'm already cold," she says.

"There's a stove over here," he tells her, beckoning, and as she notices the black pipe rising up through the low ceiling she smells the warmth. Beyond it, there's a collection of unsculpted stone, ordered by material and size. Some cut into blocks, others looking as if only the weather has ever touched them. Serpentine, soapstone, marble, argillite, quartzite, bone, antler, ivory. Jenny opens her rucksack and takes out the digital voice recorder, her notebook, and a pen, hoping the ink isn't congealed from being outside. She has a list of questions on a sheet of paper slotted into a plastic see-through file.

AFTER SHE'S INTERVIEWED HIM and Kenu has gone home for lunch, Jenny rushes back through the town to her room to type up her notes. The rushing makes her sweat and for a time she sits at her desk shivering as her body cools down. In under five hours, She'll go back to the studio to take up her dinner invitation. It will be dark then; she's glad she already knows the way.

ON HER RETURN TRIP, she realizes there must be an optimum pace at which to move. If she walks too slowly, her toes and fingers grow numb then start to ache, while if she walks too quickly she sweats and that makes her cold as soon as she stops. She looks around for other people, hard to see at first in the dull street lighting, then imitates the pace at which they are walking.

At the studio, she knocks quietly and enters wordlessly. Kenu is working on a different piece. The abstracted bear-man of the morning has been put away, or pushed away, supposes Jenny, as it must be heavy. Kenu raises one hand to acknowledge her arrival and she sits, trying to make her body look relaxed, to denote that she's happy to wait. She watches him for many minutes until he straightens up, pushes his forefingers into the base of his spine, and gently returns a mallet and a toothed chisel to the correct empty outlines on the board above the workbench. Then he hefts the lump of serpentine from the sandbag it has been resting on, places it on a sturdy shelf and drapes a cloth over it.

"I don't want its spirit to escape while I'm away," he jokes.

"I'm having trouble finding it as it is and I need it to stay inside until I've finished."

From what Jenny had seen, there's a bird spirit residing in the stone, one green wing unfolding. It reminds her of the arctic skuas she has read about. They have a cuckoo mind. Even though they can fish for themselves, they chase other birds, forcing them to drop or disgorge their catch midair, seizing it before it hits the water.

"Did you tell your mum I'm vegetarian?" Jenny asks as they walk to Kenu's house. She is trying to concentrate on the route they take so that she can find her way back. "I really don't want to be a nuisance."

"I told her. She doesn't quite understand how you can survive without meat," he laughs, "or why on earth you should want to, but," Kenu pauses, changes tone, "you see, traditionally, if you didn't eat meat you'd never have survived here. We have only really two months when you can eat plants and berries."

"Thank God for the white invasion of the north," says Jenny. "Bringing three-dollar apples and jars of peanut butter and jam."

"And white sliced bread," adds Kenu. "What's the point of PB and J without white sliced bread to roll it up in?"

They are silent for a few moments and Jenny wonders if all those emails were a bad idea. They should have saved up some words to say to each other with their voice boxes rather than their mailboxes.

The houses they are passing are small and cube-shaped, except the roofs aren't flat, they're slanted. Here, she can see the stilts that raise the houses off the ground. They look too spindly, as if they could be kicked out from under each house and it would fall over.

"Have you ever tried sculpting serpentine?" Kenu asks. "You'd love it, Jenny. It's so smooth, so forgiving. Soft as skin sometimes."

When Jenny shakes her head, he laughs. "Don't tell me academics never have a go at these things. I saw the way you were looking at my tools, my gatherings."

"Yeah, well," admits Jenny. "I did a bit when I was a child. Clay mostly, though I liked the idea of woodcarving."

"I like woodcarving," says Kenu. "I'm never sure whether to get into it or not. I mean, wood is scarce round here traditionally. But then I use non-native stone, so why don't I carve wood too?" Jenny can tell he's not intending to bring the conversation back to him. He's lending her one of his doubts as if to encourage her to lend him one of hers in return.

Jenny laughs and Kenu looks at her. "I was a bit of a disaster with woodcarving," she says. "When I was a child, about ten I think, I'd seen some photographs of some wooden sculptures in a magazine. These sculptures were abstract, very intricate but not fussy. Anyway, I went up to my bedroom that night and suddenly started noticing how much wood there was in my room, bed, bookshelves, window frames, chair, desk, and how plain it all was. So I got out my penknife — I was a bit of a tomboy — turned my chair upside-down and sat on the edge of my bed. I started carving. Whittling away at this chair leg, making what I thought was a pretty pattern."

She stops. Kenu is laughing. "That's great, really great."

"When my mum was tidying up my room a couple of days later, she noticed my chair was wobbly. I'd made that leg shorter than all the others. My parents were furious. They confiscated my penknife and I had to stuff a piece of folded-up paper under the chair leg until I could persuade my dad to saw an inch off the other three legs to even things out. Never did get that penknife back. That was the end of my sculpting career."

"Sounds like just the beginning to me," Kenu says.

SHE MUST HAVE BEEN looking out for them. The front door opens before they have walked up the wooden steps to the porch, before Kenu has had time to take his keys out of his pocket.

"Hello Manniit," she says, smiling at Jenny. Her small eyes are darker than her son's.

"Mom," Kenu says, shaking his head and turning to look at Jenny. "Manniit means egg," he explains. "It's also what we call the month of June because that's when people go out gathering eggs from the geese and ducks who migrate here. I guess it's the vegetarian month."

Jenny, giving Kenu her coat to hang up by the door, says, "June is a woman's name anyway, though I don't think egg is. Why is it you can name someone May, June, or April but not January or February?" She's talking too much. Kenu is trying to introduce her to his mother.

"This is my Mom, Ovilu," he says. Jenny holds out her hand and they clutch each other's fingers briefly. "So, Mom, what's for dinner?"

"We're all vegetarian tonight. Char for everyone."

Jenny closes her eyes quickly, then, opening them, tries to make them look kind. "I'm so sorry," she says. "I don't eat fish."

Ovilu looks bewildered. "Fish isn't meat," she says.

"I'm so sorry."

"You don't eat fish?" Kenu looks at her.

"I'm afraid not." They're both staring at her. "To eat a fish, you have to kill it. And I couldn't, can't kill anything, so I don't ask that anyone else does it for me. Does that make sense? I really am sorry. I can just eat some bread or something. Peanut butter and jam," she smiles at Kenu. "I'll be fine."

They leave Jenny standing in the front room and go through to the kitchen together, speaking quietly in Inuktitut. Jenny thinks of leaving the house while they are out of the room. She thinks of offering to go when they come back in. Then, remembering her research, she looks around for a way to show that she's making herself at home. She has read that this is how to honour Inuit people in their own tradition. Easy to read about. Harder when you're standing in someone's front room which doesn't truthfully look any different from any others in

North America. She gets up and goes to a small bookcase, tilts her head to read the titles. There's a row of crime novels, well-read paperbacks with disintegrating spines. Patricia Cornwell, Minette Walters. A couple of Agatha Christies. Jenny slides *From Potter's Field* from the shelf, sits on the settee, and tries to start reading.

As soon as she hears them coming back into the room she snaps the book shut and stands up. Ovilu, face as fixed as a photograph, is carrying a wide-bottomed shallow dish, and Kenu brings in a tray with slices of white bread in a basket, a block of cheese, butter, and two large jars of peanut butter and blueberry jam. Ovilu nods at Jenny to sit at the table and when Jenny does she realizes she's still got the novel in her hand. She places it in the small space between her buttocks and the back of the chair.

"We don't eat as much meat as we used to, or fish," Ovilu says, sitting down gently, her face relaxing. 'This is arctic char." She points a finger at a dish. "My old friends sometimes bring me country food but their sons don't hunt so much now. Too busy with government programs."

"Country food is what we call, um, hunted food. Our native food." says Kenu.

"Yes, so I've heard," Jenny said. Better, probably, to say heard than read. "And typical country food would be caribou? Seal?" she asks, deciding to learn what she thinks she already knows.

"Yes," Ovilu says with her first smile since calling Jenny Manniit.

The book behind Jenny on the chair slips off and slaps the floor. "Sorry," whispers Jenny, and twists round and down to pick it up. She changes her mind and slides it under the chair instead.

"Mom is a great cook," Kenu said, giving Jenny a grin as she sits upright, face flushed.

"Not a great cook. A listening cook. I paid attention to my elders, remembered what they taught me. But the word 'cook' it is not the right word," says Ovilu with a glance at Kenu, who sighs.

"You mean, you don't traditionally cook your food?" Jenny says.

"That's right," says Ovilu. "It's sad. You will never taste *aalu*."

"Ah-loo?" Jenny tries to repeat it.

"I don't think you want to know," Kenu says.

"*Aalu*. Delicious. Caribou or seal, though best with seal. Seal is always best. Whatever, the meat must be clean and lean. Cut it up into tiny pieces then add just a few drops of melted fat, then a few drops of blood. Then add *uruniq*."

"You really don't want to know." Kenu is laughing.

Jenny looks at Ovilu.

"The intestine of ptarmigan," she explains, obsidian-eyed. "Use your fingers to stir it all up until it's fluffy. Delicious. Very popular."

There's a warm gleam in Ovilu's eyes now, like an ooze of fresh blood. "We never imprison animals like your people do. We are never cruel."

"No," Jenny says. She looks down and starts to spread peanut butter on a slice of bread.

"So," says Ovilu after a few quiet mouthfuls of char. "You're studying my son?"

"Yes, and other artists. Sculptors."

"That's why you're here?"

"Yes."

"Even though you are vegetarian, it's okay for people to carve bone, ivory, antler?"

"I'm mostly interested in stone but, yes, I study other materials too. I have to be thorough."

"Isn't that hypocritical?"

"Mom," warns Kenu.

"Yes," Jenny says. "It is hypocritical." She won't win an argument with this woman but she can at least be honest. "But I have to be vegetarian, it's my way, and I want to study your art, your carving. I don't know why, I just do."

Ovilu looks at Jenny. "Okay," she says.

"I don't have any answers," Jenny says.

Ovilu takes another quick mouthful of char. "You are paid? Paid to be here?"

"Kind of. A research grant. It's not much, I have to work too when I'm home."

Ovilu laughs. "It's funny. You're paid to study our art."

Jenny says nothing.

"And yet, there's so little of it."

Jenny waits.

"There's so little genuine Inuit art in your western sense, isn't there?" Ovilu waves her hand in the air as if she could create art by magic.

"Mom, we've had this conversation a hundred times," interrupts Kenu. "Anyway, Jenny has studied other art, too, First Nation, and she's interested in our whole culture, how our arts developed. Where it came from. Why things are as they are now."

Yes, thinks Jenny. He explains it well.

"We didn't create art for its own sake," Ovilu says, talking with her mouth full. "We made harpoon handles and pots and combs and we decorated them. Or we carved the wand the shaman used or amulets for us to wear to protect us from the bad spirits." She stopped to swallow. "We carved tiny trinkets to trade with your people. That was their purpose. Everything had a purpose. Not like your art. You think if it has a purpose then it isn't art. The artist communities that we have now, that your people have given us. They just create prettinesses to sell to the visitors. They don't even use traditional ways. My son. What do I do with the sculptures he gives me?"

Jenny knows she's going to have to say something.

"Tell me, Manniit," Ovilu continues. "What use are my son's sculptures? Pretty enough. Heavy enough, some of them, but too big for paperweights."

"Art doesn't have to have a function in the conventional sense." Jenny looks down at the bread on her plate. "Expressing creativity is a function in itself. People still have an urge to create, even when their basic needs are met, especially when their basic needs are met. It's not just about tools and clothes. Sculpture, print-making, sewing. It gives talented people an outlet. And you might not know or care, but your son is brilliant." Jenny pauses, glances at Ovilu but her face is placid. Jenny decides to be bold. "Why did you have a son? You didn't need a child to support you, the government is now there to do that. Having a family is a form of creativity, too."

Ovilu smiles at Kenu. "You know, she's better at this than you are, but then she ought to be. She's gets paid to watch it being done while you get paid to actually do it."

KENU WALKS JENNY HOME to the research centre even though she's tried to persuade him not to; she doesn't want him to apologize for his mother, as she knows he will, because his mother is right. Jenny is worse, perhaps, than the first white men to come here. They at least traded goods, things that were wanted: steel needles, copper kettles, and iron-bladed knives in exchange for sealskin clothes and delicate bone carvings. And other things, too, it's true. Tobacco and alcohol, things they could have done without.

Yet she trades nothing, only takes.

Takes notes and photographs, kidnaps ideas and gives birth to stillborn inspiration. Won't even eat their food.

WHEN KENU HAS LEFT HER at the door to the building, Jenny goes quietly to her room. Inside, without removing her outdoor clothes, she feels in her pocket and takes out her penknife. She reaches down for the wooden chair at her desk and twists it upside down with one hand. Then she sits down on the bed, wedges a chair leg between her knees, and digs her knife into the varnished wood.

Machair

As soon as it slithered out of its birth goo, Helen could see that the lamb was a short-jaw. Absurdly, her first response — instinct, perhaps — was to hide it. The back of the barn. The shed. The spare bedroom.

She could see, too, from the way it licked the orifices and surfaces of the lamb, sucking up the mucilage, that the ewe was going to be a good mother. Watching, Helen sat back on her heels then twisted her bottom onto the muddied concrete floor, remembering that only children, not fifty-seven-year-olds, could sit on their heels for more than a few minutes. She was waiting for the ewe to judder again and deliver the twin. For there was a twin, Helen knew.

There was a dim light above and below the barn door, as if someone had taken the lid off the night and then hadn't put it back on properly. She looked at her watch. Approaching four. Only another hour to go then it would be David's turn, thank God. As well as a coat and hat, she was wearing two fleeces, but these human-made imitations of sheep's clothing were obviously nowhere near as effective at keeping out the cold as the genuine article. Tomorrow night, David could freeze on the graveyard shift. After all, it had been his idea to transform their three decades of annual visits to Sutherland into permanent residence. Not that she hadn't agreed. Indeed, she'd been the one to organize everything. Someone had to and it wasn't going to be David.

Bugger. The second twin was a short-jaw too. So this would be the extent of this young ewe's experience of maternity. A short-jaw herself, though bred from a normal ewe, she'd failed the test. Neither twin had any chance of being a breeder, either. Straight to slaughter once they were heavy enough. Not that Helen believed having a shorter jaw had impeded the ewe in any way. She could masticate effectively. No signs of nutrient deficiency. A good breeder if it wasn't for this superficial defect. Not even a defect, actually. Merely an aesthetic shortcoming. Helen wouldn't have thought farmers worried about aesthetics, but after three years of crofting she and her husband had learnt how important the look of an animal was.

HELEN TORE OFF A PIECE of her buttered crust and dropped it to the floor. She knew Molly, the youngest of their three sheepdogs, would be under the table, which was confirmed by sounds of crunching.

"She's a good mother, that ewe," David said. "Waste of three potentially good breeders. We'd better get a good slaughter price for them."

He scraped his knife against the bottom of the marmalade jar to scoop up the last sliver of rind. Helen didn't know how he could eat marmalade. It was jam made with the wrong fruit. Lambing was over. That was why she and her husband could have breakfast together, not that they hadn't both been up since five this morning. Their third season had been a good one and it was keeping them busy; thirty-eight lambs in total.

"You don't think it's worth one more try," Helen said. "Give her another season?"

David shook his head, swallowing a mouthful of toast. "Better to cut our losses. Put the slaughter money toward another ewe." He looked at his wife. "You're not turning soft in your old age, I hope."

It was only after she had stood up and carried her plate and mug over to the sink that Helen responded. "I just don't consider having a short jaw to be a handicap."

"Are you allowed to say handicap any more?" David mused. "Mandibularly challenged, I should think is what you're supposed to say."

Helen couldn't smile at his joke. "It doesn't affect her breeding —"

"Except she's perpetuating the short-jaw gene," interrupted David.

"It doesn't affect her feeding or motherhood. And the twins are bleating and baa-ing as well as the rest of them. Farmers and finishers don't like them simply because they look different."

"You're right, darling. But we crofters are merely the servants of such esteemed folk."

In the days after the lambs were born, the machair bloomed and Helen took to walking across it daily between chores to the gold crescent of the bay. It was impossible to walk without treading on any of the flowers. It was impossible to move without crunching the thousands of shells that lay within and on top of the sandy soil, making her feel like a cruel queen who demanded beauty and excess and then destroyed them both.

Today, in order to escape crushing an orchid, she trod on a gentian by mistake and winced. She evidently couldn't watch where she stepped while also keeping an eye out for the Scots primrose's first bloom of the year. For the past three summers she'd only caught them in July, well into their second florescence. The only way she was going to spot one now was to stand still and look, but she found herself unable to stop her steady movement toward the sea.

When she reached the beach, Helen took off her boots and socks and bathed her feet in the white frills of lace at the turquoise water's edge. The water was freezing, the veins in her feet and ankles throbbing as they contracted with the cold. It would do her good. She would stay in the water until she had come to her senses.

She hadn't mentioned it again to David but her mind was saturated with thoughts of the ewe and the twin short-jaws.

It was clear why. The simplicity of it was a psychiatrist's dream.

A woman whose life was made a misery as a child for having a handicap. She suppresses the experience until she's menopausal, then makes a fool of herself over three mildly deformed sheep that have to go to the slaughterhouse. Even though they would be going to slaughter sooner or later anyway, and were simply going to be stunned and cut rather earlier than usual.

The child and sheep shared, of course, the same handicap.

BY NOW, THE PAIN IN HER FEET was unbearable. Helen ran out of the water, picked up her boots and socks and climbed up onto a bonsai mountain of granite, glad no one could see her broad-bottomed clambering. The rocks had a flat slab on top and an almost flat upright surface that served very well as a backrest. She didn't care if she was too old to be scrambling up rocks.

The wind, ever present, was tugging at a crop of papery pink thrift anchored in a sandy crevice. Helen decided she would rather be thrift, here on the rock face and splashed by the turning tide, than an orchid safely rooted behind the dunes on the machair. She rubbed her feet with both hands, enjoying the friction of sand between her toes which she knew would leave a speckled deposit when she drained her evening bath.

She really should try and forget the damn ewe and its lambs. Be her customary pragmatic self. Breed them or eat them; that was how it was.

WHEN SHE WAS NINE, a doctor had told Helen that nothing could be done about her deformity; she would have it her whole life. Defect, he'd corrected himself, was perhaps a more appropriate word than deformity. She shouldn't make a fuss; it could have been a lot worse. He suggested that she might prefer to concentrate on her school work rather than on her looks and future marriage prospects. This defect, as the doctor had termed it, was that her lower jaw hung out too far, like an opened drawer that had warped and couldn't be slid shut.

It was her English teacher, Mrs. Wilson, who had noticed that while Helen's written work was excellent she never said a word in class and didn't appear to have any friends. She gained the permission of Helen's parents to take Helen to a surgeon colleague of her husband. Three operations and an incremental adjustment of muscle and tendon later, Helen was showing off her scars to new friends rather than keeping her head dipped and avoiding talking to anyone. By the time Helen met David, when they were both twenty-one, her jaws were almost perfectly matched. It might have been the nineteen-sixties when Helen first brought her future husband home but, as far as her parents were concerned, reticence and discretion were still society's dominant mores. Neither they nor Helen had ever told David about her childhood operations; there hadn't been any need.

David had accepted her decision to have a full-time career as a teacher instead of a brood of children; she'd never had to reveal her deformity or her fear that it was hereditary. In fact, she believed he'd enjoyed not having to share her with anyone except their dogs, cats, and friends. He wouldn't have expected her to keep anything secret from him, because he didn't appear to keep anything secret from her.

Even when he had his nervous breakdown, just four years ago, he did it publicly. When the police brought him home after they picked him up riding his bicycle along the hard shoulder of the motorway, he'd apparently chattered so liberally during the journey in the panda car — if that was what they were still called — that the police had told her he was probably lonely. Probably just needed more of her attention rather than a psychiatrist. She'd tried not to laugh at that. He'd had her attention all the thirty years of their married life. To have given him any more attention would have been like turning herself from convex to concave, or from three dimensions into two. Even so, she had tried. She had encouraged his idea to take early retirement and move from Surrey to Sutherland. She had found the house and land that they bought, making sure she understood the Scottish house-selling system, and negotiated with David's boss for his early retirement and a silver, if not a golden, handshake. And she had informed their bemused families and friends of their plans and absorbed their critical, sarcastic, and even jealous comments so efficiently he knew nothing of them.

BEFORE SHE RETURNED to the house, Helen went into the barn and to the pen where the short-jaw ewe and her two lambs lay. She watched the lambs suckling for a long time. She had been right; the ewe was a good mother. There was no need to worry.

Inside the house, Helen threw her damp socks into the washing machine and employed herself with the secret, womanly things that she only did when she knew David couldn't see her. Straightening cushions and curtains, wiping the sideboard after he'd already attempted to clear his lunch crumbs. Largely pointless in a sense, she knew, because the overpowering impression that anyone received on entering the cottage was olfactory, not visual. It was dog. And dog signified uncleanliness, regardless of how tidy their home was. It was the cumulative aroma of the three sheepdogs — one dying — who were supposed to sleep in the shed but never did because both she and her husband were too sentimental.

Noticing that David had left an empty mug on the table beside his armchair, Helen went into the sitting room to pick it up. The moment it was in her grasp she couldn't hold it. She hurled it through the door to the kitchen, down onto the liver-red quarry tiles.

Before David and the dogs came in from the fields, she swept up the fragments of china and slid them from the dustpan into the pedal bin. Once that was done and even though it was supper-time and she hadn't prepared anything, she put on a clean pair of socks and the same boots and walked back across the machair to the beach.

The end of the summer was nearing. Helen was coming in from her last walk of the day. As she removed her boots, she could smell that David was cooking. It didn't smell like beans on toast or baked potatoes, either, the easy things that he'd been preparing for them since she'd stopped cooking.

"Darling, sit down, supper's almost ready," David said.

Helen held out her hands. "Let me have a wash first. I'm all sea-salty."

When she was ready he set their plates on the table. "There you go."

Meat, new potatoes, and French beans. An entirely different menu.

David nodded at Helen to start eating as he sat down opposite her.

It was delicious. She had been right to let him take care of the cooking lately. It was time he realized how much she'd done for him over the years. It was true she hadn't been helping as much with the farming, either. He looked tired but he seemed to be managing.

"Lamb chops." David smiled. "Our very own, too."

Helen, mouth full, paused. "How so?"

"It's the short-jaw ewe. I had her slaughtered as a one-off. They did a marvellous job — sent her back in vacuum-packed single portions for the freezer. Ideal for couples on their own like us."

Helen put down her fork.

"You've been so, well, preoccupied lately." David put his cutlery down, too. "I didn't want to bother you. We agreed, didn't we? That they'd all go to slaughter, the three short-jaws, that we couldn't breed them."

Helen pushed back her chair and stood up. She went to the window that overlooked the top field. "The lambs too?" she asked.

"They've not gone yet, no. They're still fattening."

Turning to her husband, Helen opened her mouth. As she waited for the words to flow, she visualised a wave breaking on the beach. "There's something I want to say to you."

David leant forward as if he was going to stand up but he remained seated. She turned back to the window.

"You can't." David said. "Not after all this time. Not after putting up with me for so long. I can't cope without you, you know that. You just need a longer break. I'll carry on doing the cooking forever if you like. I'll take on all the chores."

Helen turned back to him. He had risen from his chair but he hadn't moved towards her. "Silly billy." She made herself smile. "What I want to say is that you're not going to send the short-jaw lambs to slaughter. We're going to keep them."

"Okay, fair enough. Whatever you want."

"I'm a short-jaw too. You never knew that, did you?"

David stepped towards her, frowning. "What do you mean?"

"Overbite," Helen said, flapping a hand towards her face. "Corrected as a child."

David was going to say more but she didn't let him.

"Looks aren't everything, for heaven's sake." She sat back down at the table and David did, too. "We'll damn well breed those lambs," she told him. "There's absolutely nothing wrong with them and we'll prove it."

The World's First Spin Doctor

THREE HUNDRED AND TWENTY MILLION YEARS AGO, BATHGATE in central Scotland was on the equator. There are fossils on the edge of the town that prove it. Anyone who has ever been to Bathgate is likely to find this amusing. It's more of an unemployment blackspot than a holiday hotspot. No one at Rob Munro's school in London had a clue what Bathgate was like. They thought it was funny enough that he went on holiday every summer to Scotland when they were all going off to the Costa del Sol or Majorca. He used to imagine telling them, "Actually, I'm going to the equator." Of course, he never did.

The reason Rob went up to Bathgate from London every summer was because that was where his nan and granddad stayed, up on the scheme by the old limestone quarry, where the Bathgate hills start their hiccups. Except he couldn't say "stayed" when he told people at school where he was going; he had to speak English, not Scottish, and say Bathgate was where his nan and granddad "lived." He'd said stayed by accident once and had been teased about it for weeks.

Rob and his mum loved to get away. They hated London. "It's too big. It's obese. It needs to go on a diet," his mum would say. His dad never went with them; he was too busy running his minicab firm. He was good. Good driver. Good boss. Greenock-born, he knew London better than any Cockney.

Sedulously rather than genetically, he passed on his A to Z knowledge of London streets to his son. But Rob would rather not possess this directory of information. Even now, at work in Edinburgh, whenever his colleagues start arguing about the best route to take from King's Cross to their London branch, he stands and offers to make coffee. He hurries to the kitchen to swallow his father's pride.

While he doesn't want his father's cartographical knowledge of England's capital, Rob does wish he had his father's accent. If only his dad had bequeathed him his voice box, rather than a garage of gear boxes and a box of London A to Z maps that includes a first edition from 1936. There's no English blood in Rob, as far as he knows, yet he sounds English. His accent is formed of sedimentary layers. First, a fragile layer of Scottish laid down by babyish mimicry of his parents' voices that isn't even perceptible when he's drunk. Next, the estuary English he learnt from his friends at school. Then the layer he deposited at sixth-form college, when he decided that the middle-class boys sounded more intelligent. The final layer is the Edinburgh accent he's been trying to deposit for the seven years he's lived in Scotland. But the soil is light and wind and rain continually remove it. People say it's hard to learn a second language, but it's even more difficult to learn to change the way you speak your first language.

He might crave a Scottish accent but Rob isn't purely Scottish. He's part Viking. He knows he is, even though no one, as far as he's aware, has ever dug into Munro genealogy. Rob himself doesn't need to visit the General Register Office. He knew it the moment he picked up a chunk of sandstone on the island the Vikings called Orkneyjar. It's as if he made that journey two years ago specifically to collect that rock, left there for him ten centuries earlier by his Viking ancestors.

He'd come across the stone when he took a short cut to the cliffs for a better look at the famous sea stack, the Old Man of Hoy. As soon as he picked it up he knew he'd found something.

Something he hadn't realized he'd lost. More important than finding a sock under the washing machine. More like finding a twenty-pound note between a bunch of receipts you're about to chuck in the bucket.

Rob believes the stone is an artefact; there's a groove around its flat edges that nature couldn't have carved. Even though he can't work out what the stone was used for, he can see how a rope could be eased into the groove.

He's certain he's a Viking. He's big, and he's got that reddish-blond skin that burns easily. As soon as he understood his provenance, he realized he had always felt like a cake that has cooked too quickly, leaving the inside still soggy; he looked like a fully formed person to everyone who saw him, yet he'd always felt unfinished, uncertain, unclassified. That was probably why he was in public relations; he knew how to make things look good on the outside.

He's holding the stone now. He often picks up the small trapezoid and carries it around his house when he's nervous. It's the party in Edinburgh that's making him nervous tonight. And excited. Nervous because he hates entering parties on his own. He gets a panic attack if he doesn't see someone he knows within nine seconds; he's counted. Excited because the woman of his dreams might be there.

He has to put the stone down to change his clothes. He finds a clean top in a drawer and shakes it to see if he can get away without ironing it. No, he can't. He sets up the ironing board at the end of the bed and plugs in the iron. While he's waiting for it to heat, he takes a pair of jeans out of the chest of drawers and puts them on. They're creased but it doesn't matter with jeans, surely.

The only time he ever looked forward to a party was the fancy dress do Maggie had last year when he'd gone, naturally, as a Viking. People kept asking him where his helmet and horns were. He'd explained that it was a myth that Vikings wore such things. Maggie, when she saw him in his plaits (his hair was longer then), tunic, hose, and cloak, said she was glad he'd decided to come out of the closet at last.

He and Maggie had been going out back then but it hadn't lasted long after the party, and not because of the Viking outfit. She said she was sick of him. He never wanted to do anything. Normal things like shopping, eating out, going to the cinema. She'd even called him a miser and accused him of hoarding his money. This isn't true; he spends money. Mostly on books, about Scottish history, ancient history, Viking history. And he spends money on trips up north. But Maggie hated travelling for hours just, as she put it, to look at a pile of stones or lumps in the ground. Even brochs hadn't impressed her. What Maggie wanted him to spend his money on was taking her to restaurants and holidays in hot places. She likes Spain. The Greek Islands. She isn't unusual.

Maggie enjoys giving parties, like the one tonight. They're still friends, which is why he's invited.

The iron is hot enough now. He isn't sure he's picked the right shirt to wear. Grey had looked sophisticated when he'd bought it. Now it looks middle-aged. He irons the shirt as quickly as he can and puts it on. He opens the door of his wardrobe and takes out his Viking cloak. He loves the weight of it, the imaginary tug of mud on its hem. Then he puts it away again and goes downstairs to get his coat.

IT'S MAGGIE HE SEES FIRST because she opens the door. There will be no panic attack now. Maggie tweezers his forearm between her thumb and fingers and places him inside a conversation. As if it's that simple to unclasp the conversational hands of the people he's standing between. A woman is looking at him. She smiles and he likes her face. He likes her clothes, too. The layers she is wearing are difficult to define. She has a long cardigan, over a shirt, over a further long top of some kind. And her trousers are wide and don't quite reach her ankles, revealing white flesh above her socks and boots. There is a solid largeness about her that he admires, envies in fact because his own largeness isn't solid at all.

"This is Kim," Maggie is saying. "Kim, this is Rob. He can speak. On a good day."

Maggie stays and helps him talk to Kim, like a parent holding the wrist of a child learning to play table tennis. After several minutes, mid-swing, Rob realizes Maggie has gone, leaving him to tap the ball back over the net on his own. He hits too hard.

"Would you like to dance?" he says. Surely the ping-pong ball will miss the table and bounce onto the floor.

"I hate dancing," Kim says.

"So do I." Rob giggles. It must be nerves that make him laugh; he's only had half a beer. Kim giggles back and the surprise of this emboldens him.

"We could dance ironically," he suggests. "Or just badly."

"I'm good at badly," Kim says, and they walk together to the other end of the room where dark bodies are moving.

When a slower song starts playing, Rob reaches his arms towards Kim, hoping that she is as solid as she looks.

"Wait," she says. "I'm hot."

She wriggles off her cardigan and walks a couple of steps away to drape it on a chair. Her arms are bare now and she is wearing a bracelet around her left upper arm.

"Badly isn't good enough," Kim says, returning. "I can't stand this noise. Let's get another drink and find a quieter room."

As he follows, Rob sees that her bracelet has the head of some open-jawed animal at each end.

"I like your bracelet," he says, nodding at her arm once they have sat down on some cushions on the floor.

"It's an armlet," Kim says.

"It looks —" Rob hesitates. He wants to say the word "Viking" but it feels like swearing if he uses the word inappropriately. Worse than swearing; he swears all the time.

"It's from Greenland," Kim interrupts his pause. "It's Viking."

Maggie, of course, has put her up to it. He raises his eyebrows.

"Why that funny look?"

"I know what you're doing," Rob says.

"What?"

"People think it's funny that I'm into Vikings."

"Are you?" Kim says. "I didn't know. I like Vikings, too. Their mythology. I've studied them a bit. I'm doing anthropology at university."

She's a good actress or she's telling the truth. She said the armlet was from Greenland. People usually think of Scandinavia when they think of Vikings, not Greenland. People don't think anyone lives in Greenland, or ever did.

"How did you get it?" he says. He takes a swig of beer and spills some down his shirt. He pretends not to notice and hopes Kim hasn't, either.

"Not in Greenland. I bought it from a shop in Victoria Street. It's only a replica."

"Eric the Red," Rob says, "was the world's first spin doctor."

"I know," Kim says. "He gave Greenland its name. Called it Greenland rather than what he should have called it which was A-land-of-ice-and-snow-and-we"ll-all-mysteriously-die-out-in-a-few-hundred-years."

She knows about Vikings and Greenland. How Eric the Red persuaded hundreds of people to travel there with him to settle.

"Is that what got you into PR?" asks Kim. "Maggie told me that's what you do."

Rob considers the question.

"No," he says. "I've been in public relations since I was nineteen, since I came to Edinburgh, and I didn't know about Vikings or Eric the Red then."

"I'd love to retrace their steps," Kim says. "Go to Orkney, Norway, Iceland. Greenland."

"A grand tour." Rob laughs.

"See the midnight sun. Or the northern lights."

"See Erik the Red's house."

"The church his wife had built."

She knows her stuff.

"Would you?" he asks.

"Would I what?"

"Go to Greenland. With me. Would you come with me to Greenland?"

Kim's eyes, looking at his, are the colour of snow shadows. "Yes," she says, leaning forward and kissing him quickly on the lips. "Yes."

WHEN KIM GETS UP to get them both another drink, Rob rises from the cushions and follows her. He sees her find Maggie in another room and observes the two women as they talk. He watches Kim twist her armlet and sees Maggie look at it and laugh. He knows Maggie's face well. He's slept within millimetres of it, often. When Kim returns he is sitting back on the cushions. They talk for another half an hour or so about the Vikings and Greenland and Kim's anthropological studies. How it's apparently true that the valleys in southern Greenland were grassier back then, that Eric the Red, to be fair, couldn't have known that the climate would alter.

Rob is tired now. He tells Kim he's knackered and must go home. She kisses him again, more slowly.

"Got a pen?" she says, afterwards.

He always has it on him, his Greenland pen. It has the national flag on it. A red and white circle on a red and white background curving round the pen shaft. It took ages to find on eBay. He takes it out of his jeans' pocket and hands it to her. She doesn't recognise the Greenland flag, he's sure of it.

Kim finds a receipt in her bag and leans on the table in the hallway to write down her mobile number and email address. She gives Rob the receipt and slips the pen into her bag. She's looking at him while she's doing it but he can't tell what she's thinking. She leans forward to kiss him again; he leans back.

"Can I have it back?" Rob says.

"What?"

"The pen. My pen."

"Oh." Kim rummages in her bag then holds the pen out to him. "I wasn't thinking."

When she kisses him on the lips to say goodbye, Rob keeps his lips closed.

As he drives home alone along the M8, Rob tries to remember what else they talked about apart from Vikings. Did he tell her he stays in Bathgate? He lives outside Edinburgh because it means he can afford a whole house and garden rather than a flat and he likes being on the edge of the countryside. His house, with its steep chalet roof and wood cladding, would look more interesting if it was on its own but it is one in a row of seven, each backing onto the disused limestone quarry.

He still likes to go looking for fossils there that prove the land was on the equator many million years ago. He remembers the little silver hammer his nan gave him with a tray of toffee after a week in Adrossan. He used the hammer, after the toffee was consumed, to chip out the fossilised spaghetti he found so much of at the quarry. There was an old man there once, with a proper hammer and chisel in a canvas rucksack, and he told Rob that the spaghetti was really the stems of sea lilies — crinoids —from the early Carboniferous period. He told him that the world's oldest known reptile had been found in this quarry. It was called *westlothiana lizzii*, after the place in which it was discovered. When Rob ran home and told his mum and his nan this they laughed and told him the old man had been having him on. He was grown up before he discovered the old man had been telling the truth.

Rob is glad he discovered fossiling so early in his life; it's made him observant, attentive to details.

WHEN HE ARRIVES HOME and opens the front door Rob imagines, momentarily, he has brought Kim home. Women usually like his house; they are surprised at his neatness and they like the earth colours he lives between. He is not a cruel person, merely self-preserving.

Before he takes his coat off he goes into the kitchen to switch on the kettle and into the lounge to switch on the computer. As the computer whirrs, he removes his coat and shoes then makes a cup of instant hot chocolate. Putting the drink down on the desk, he takes the receipt that Kim wrote her number on from his pocket and tears it into tiny pieces. He scoops the pieces into his hand and takes them into the kitchen where he drops them into the little compost bin he keeps on the counter. He doesn't grow vegetables yet but he will one day. For now, he uses the compost for the heather, harebells, and bog myrtle in his garden.

It isn't difficult to find a list of websites offering flights to Greenland. He checks his diary and chooses an outward and a return date. He should be able to get three weeks off work, even at short notice; he's been there long enough. The next box that he has to fill in asks him how many people are travelling. He slides the mouse along the options and clicks to select "one."

Death on the Wing

FROG-LEGGING HER FEET TO COOL PATCHES OF SHEET, MAIRI feels for the weight of Henry's body lying on top of the bed-spread, but her black Labrador isn't there. She's emerged from her dream with a sensation that she's missed something. Was it the exhalation of the bedsprings as the dog eased himself off the mattress that woke her? She doesn't like sleeping without Henry. It isn't sentimentality; she just hasn't got anyone else to sleep with at the moment.

Twelve minutes past two, the hour for sleep or sex. Nothing else, unless she's on duty.

Shit. That's where she should be, checking the peregrines. It's Saturday, well, Sunday morning, the last night of her shift. She'd only planned a quick snooze. She'd better get over there.

She expects Henry to come through the bedroom door when she switches on the light, but he doesn't. She remembers now. Henry found something interesting in the garden just before she came in and she left him outside. She unlocks the front door but Henry still isn't ready to come in. She dresses and cleans her teeth to help her wake up. Once her coat is on, she shrugs on the backpack that already contains a rope and harness, just in case she has to climb down the gorge. She likes to be ready for anything.

OUTSIDE, MAIRI CALLS HENRY'S NAME, low and soft, and waits for several moments. There's no response; he loves being out at night, loves it when she's on watch, a walk every hour or so. He'll have to catch her up.

By lifting her boots and placing her weight more on the front part of her feet she can minimize the noise of swishing leaves and the snapping of twigs and branches. It's a skill she's developed over the years. Mud sucks at her heels and she wishes she'd tied her shoelaces tighter. She can smell sweet pine resin and detects the musky whiff of badger, too, not as pungent as fox. Monochromatic moonlight means she doesn't need a torch. She hardly ever does; she's known for her infrared night vision.

She can't imagine how she'd feel if the scrape was raided or if the adults were poisoned. Poisoning is easy, if you know how to get hold of an illegal pesticide like carbofuran and don't mind slashing open a rabbit to use as a plate. Stealing the eggs takes more skill, seeing as peregrine falcons are sensible enough to nest on rocky ledges.

The best way to protect them is not let anyone know they're here. She lobbied and the trust made the right decision. Keep it quiet this year at least, maybe go public next year. Time to get the security sorted and prepare for the flocks of twitchers that will no doubt alight, possibly with a thief among them, using the feather lovers as camouflage.

She'll be there soon; the barley-sugar night glow of the town across the valley is mingling with the moonlight and she knows exactly where she is. She loves the dark, never feels scared.

She's close now. She tries to subsume her movements, her noises, her smell, into the breeze, the trees and the leaves. As she nears the edge of the gorge the sound of the river drilling through it is so loud she can't tell how much noise her body is making any more. She pauses by a beech tree near the edge of the gorge, one hand on its cool elephant bark. The scrape is a dozen feet ahead of her, then fifteen or so feet down the cliff.

She's glad she stopped. There's someone there. She moves nearer , stepping behind another beech tree. He looks like a cat burglar, all in black with a harness strapped around his waist. Bastard. He's tying a climbing rope round an oak trunk. He's quick. He knows what he's doing.

Deep breath. What's the plan? Where the hell is Henry? He could scare just about anyone off. As she watches, the man clips the rope to his harness and walks towards the edge of the cliff, pulling the rope taut as he goes. There's a backpack lying on the ground but there are no clues to which type he is: killer or thief. Smash the eggs or steal them, either way the chicks die. She wishes she were a peregrine, swooping and stooping with fatal talons.

Mairi doesn't think any more. She starts running towards the man in black, raising both arms in attack and self-defence. He's turning, moving back from the edge.

"You bastard. What the hell are you doing?"

"Don't get your knickers in a twist," he says. "Just a little nocturnal gorge climbing. The latest adrenalin sport."

"Stop fucking around. I know what you're up to and I'm going to call the police."

"Feel free, I'm doing nothing wrong. This land's not private. No law against taking a wee bit of night-time exercise."

He should be running, but he's not even scared. He's either trying to poison the peregrines to protect his pigeons or he's stealing eggs for some perverse collection. Does he think that in court it'll be her word against his and there won't be enough evidence? Or has he got a pal, creeping up behind her right now? Jesus, where's Henry?

Watching him as he unclips his harness and steps out of it, she slides a hand into each pocket to find her mobile phone. Shit. It isn't there. She's left it at home. The signal is often crap here, anyway. At least she's stopped him, unless he's already set poison. Maybe she should let him get away, follow him to his car and make a note of his number plate.

"You shouldn't be out on your own in the middle of the night like this, sweetheart." His voice is thick. He sounds drunk.

"I know this place better than you ever will."

He's laughing again. "Silly bitch. I'd say it was time you were back in bed servicing your hubby. Oh, I forgot, no one wants to live with a cow like you who can't mind her own business."

She steps forward and grabs at the backpack now hooked on his shoulder. She's caught him off guard and manages to wrench it off him.

"The next time you'll see this will be in court," she shouts. There must be something in it to give his game away.

He's laughing, but he's also moving forward and for a moment she's afraid he's going to head-butt her. Instead, he embraces her in a brutal hug, trying to get his backpack. She turns her shoulders and manages to free one arm. She pulls the backpack down to her side and tosses it with an elbow twist towards the gorge.

It lands a foot from the cliff edge.

The man grunts and doesn't seem to know whether to go for the backpack or for her. He goes for the backpack and she's level with him, breathing hard. She gets there first, sliding, skidding, and slapping the ground. She scoops the backpack over the edge.

Neither of them can have it now.

"You fucking cow. I've lost eleven pigeons to your falcons."

She's moving back from the edge, still on the ground, when he kicks her ribs. The pain is sharp and she's winded.

It won't stop her, though. She wriggles away from the edge. He looms close again as if to give her another kick. "Time I was off," he says instead. "Nice meeting you."

He's not going to get away. She's up on her feet by the time he's turned around and she's shoving him hard.

He topples but there's no thud as he hits the ground, because there's no ground for him to hit. Instead, there's a shout. He's gone over, down into the gorge. A seventy-foot drop, give or take.

Jesus.

The clamour of the gushing river buries the sound of a body hitting rock.

Self-defence.

What if he'd kicked her again and she'd gone over the edge instead of him? Okay, so he'd turned his back on her and was walking away, but how could she know he wasn't going to attack her again?

Staying low, she crawls to the edge of the cliff, clutching brittle heather, and looks down. She can't see a thing. The slabs of vertical rock seem to absorb rather than refract the moonlight. Sliding the backpack off, she takes out her torch and shines it into the gorge. It makes no difference; it's still as black as a cave.

RUNNING BACK TO HER HOUSE, she doesn't care now how much noise she makes. All the time, she's shallow-breathing, trying not to make the fingers of her ribs splay too much because of the pain. Her ribs feel as if they've been bent in all directions. She's snapping twigs with her feet, snagging her hair on branches, leaving strands as evidence. That's all right because she won't deny she was there. Won't deny that they fought. Hell, that he'd attacked her.

She tries to recall the moment when she stopped thinking back there. No weighing of options, consequences. Her body commandeered her mind. Now, it's time to think and she's thinking hard.

Could anyone survive that fall? It's possible. She has to get to a phone. Call an ambulance. A helicopter is probably what they'll need. His body is bound to be broken, but he could still be alive.

JUMPING OVER THE FENCE as a short cut to the back door, Mairi sees a shape on the lawn, dark and gleaming in the moonlight.

She stops running; it's a familiar shape. She doesn't want to look but she has to.

It's Henry. The gleam isn't moonlight, it's blood. He's been cut. Knifed. Starting at the back of his neck, round to his throat. His fur is wet, matted. His eyes are open but he's not seeing anything. She yanks off her jacket, screws it up and presses it onto his neck. She strokes the length of his back with her other hand. He's cold, yet she's the one shivering.

A badger or a fox couldn't do this. She knows how four-legged mammals wound each other. It's a gutless attack from behind or on top. Food dropped to the ground, probably, Henry scoffing it up like he always does. Not looking. Not seeing the blade of the knife flash in the moonlight, a lunar warning unheeded, unseen.

She knows first aid. She also knows when a heart has stopped beating, when it's too late. Henry must have been here all the time, here by the back door when she went out the front. It must have happened before she'd even left the house.

Mairi doesn't believe in an eye for an eye. She really doesn't. She doesn't believe in jumping to conclusions, either. But she doesn't rush to the back door and she doesn't hurry to find her keys. She can't think of any other person except the pigeon man who would have done this.

Standing on the threshold, she pushes the door open and turns on the light. There's her mobile on the kitchen table where she must have left it. She crosses to the table in her dirty boots to make it look as if she's rushed to the phone. She stands by the table and picks up the phone. It's sticky in her hand because her fingers are gloved in Henry's blood. She bites into her lip until it hurts, until it forces her brain to think.

She stays standing at the table. She looks at the time on the phone. She thinks about Henry. He was nine. Sixty-three in dog years, at the latter end of middle-age. She'll bury him in the garden.

She looks at the time on the phone again. She counts to

ten, once, twice, three times. Then she unsticks her bloodied thumb from the phone to dial.

"Ambulance, please," she says. Her hands are shaking and she feels nauseous. She exaggerates her breathing so it sounds as if she's just been running. "There's been an accident."

The Accents of Birds

ANTONIA MAKES THEIR MEALS FROM SCRATCH, GRINDING onion seeds, crushing fresh coriander, grating ginger root. Her daughter, Cassie, sitting at the kitchen table sculpting Plasticine, can smell which curry recipe her mother is following. Cassie loves curries. Aged six, she has the palate of a thirty-year-old.

Antonia hears the scrape of Cassie's chair and turns to see her standing up. "Can I go in the garden, Mummy? Before it gets blue-dark."

"Just for a few minutes. I'm putting the rice on."

Cassie loves to run up and down the long garden path and Antonia is careful to keep the shrubs and grass on either side trimmed back. It's always wonderful to see Cassie moving without her cane, and so quickly.

"You'd never know, would you," Antonia's mother says each time she visits, standing at the kitchen window watching Cassie run.

Antonia wants to say: "Put a plant pot in her way and you'd soon bloody know." But she doesn't. Her mother knows no better. She never will.

Whenever her mother speaks about Cassie, her voice is a composite of pride, wistfulness and embarrassment. Since Cassie was born, Antonia has become good at listening to voices. She's learned she can't hide anything from her daughter; Cassie knows exactly when her mother's anger is on the cusp of humour, when her weariness is on the cusp of tears. People who can see don't realize that everyone keeps all their secrets in their voice. Antonia has to shut her eyes so she can concentrate and listen. She can only do this when she's on the telephone, of course, not face to face.

Antonia goes over to the open window and calls to tell Cassie tea is ready.

"I heard a blackbird, Mummy," says Cassie as she comes in. "And some chaffinches."

As she eats, Cassie says: "It's still blue-dark, isn't it? It's not black-dark yet. If it's black dark, does that mean I have to go to bed?"

Cassie recently learnt that the sun sets a minute or two later every day for half the year and then earlier every day for the other half, but it's hard for her to understand about stars and planets and satellites. Antonia has tried to explain by clasping Cassie's hands round oranges and apples and calling the orange the sun and the apple the moon. Yet it's difficult to imagine a burning star ninety-three million miles away when you've never seen one.

AFTER SHE HAS PUT CASSIE TO BED, Antonia turns all the lights off and moves around downstairs in darkness, finding, tidying with her fingers, toes, nose. In the sitting room, she sits on the settee, closing her eyes so that even the street lighting outside is shut out. Tomorrow she will be forced to decide whether they must move. Away from the only house Cassie has ever lived in, away from her clients, and away from her mother. Cassie needs a better school, a special school for special children with special needs. But hasn't the word specific replaced the word special, indicating that her child is not special any more? A specific school for specific children with specific needs. A school that already knows things about Cassie that will take Antonia all her life to learn.

A man called Simon North from the specific school is coming tomorrow. He will assess Cassie and decide whether to offer her a place. The school is more than a hundred miles away in York, in a different county. If Cassie attends, they will have to move and Antonia will have to find another house with a long garden path for Cassie to run up and down.

It would be a great relief to find a good school, even though there will be a new local authority to deal with. The teachers at her current school try hard but they don't have time to become experts on Cassie. They say she's artistic — as if this extra gift compensates for the one she failed to receive — and perhaps She'll become a sculptor or a musician. But Antonia doesn't care what Cassie becomes; she cares what becomes of her.

IN THE MORNING, Antonia is surprised when Simon arrives and cross at herself for being surprised. He's blind. Completely blind, Antonia suspects. Not like Cassie, but like Cassie may become. The doctors are hardly reassuring.

Once the door is closed behind him, Simon feels with his cane to find the wall. He moves closer and leans his cane against it so he can shrug off his jacket.

Antonia says suddenly, "Here, let me take that for you." She pulls the jacket off Simon's arm. "I'll hang it up here, on these hooks by the door." She realizes she's treating him how she treats Cassie whenever they are somewhere unfamiliar, giving him a running commentary. "Please," she says, hoping the anger in her voice isn't revealed. "Let me know how I'm supposed to help you, if you want help. I'm only used to dealing with Cassie. At her school, none of the other children have the same disability as her. I don't know anyone else. . . ." She watches Simon's face.

He smiles. "It makes a change to meet someone who's angry with me. Usually, it sounds as if they're on the verge of tears. With sympathy, I suppose, or relief that they're not me. I'm never quite sure which."

"I'm sorry," she says. "I'm not angry with you. I don't even know you. I'm angry because I can't help. I mean I can't really help. I can only do my best."

She stops talking because she knows that it's not only Cassie who's going to be assessed this morning; She'll be assessed, too. Schools don't want difficult parents any more than they want difficult children.

"It's fine," Simon says, sounding as if he means it. "Tell you what you could do, though, you could pass me my cane." He holds out his hand, thumb stretched away from his fingers, and Antonia places the cane gently against his palm. "So," he continues. "Where's Cassie? Sounds as if she's up in her room."

"I'll call her down," Antonia says.

"No, no. Let's go up and see her."

"Then I'll make us some coffee," Antonia says. "The stairs are straight ahead of you, sort of to the right."

She realizes her instructions are confusing, yet Simon manages to find the bottom step with his cane.

"There are fourteen stairs," Antonia tells him. She walks behind him as he goes up. After the first two steps he stops using his cane and glides his hand up the banister rail.

Cassie is sitting on the floor playing with her dolls, listening to Vivaldi's Four Seasons on a CD player, humming along.

"I'm not hot-housing her." Antonia laughs. "She loves all this classical stuff."

"Hi, Cassie," says Simon, bending down. "Vivaldi, eh? Are you a Nigel Kennedy fan or more of a purist?"

"More of a purist," repeats Cassie. Simon and Antonia laugh.

Antonia asks Cassie to take Simon down to the sitting room while she goes to the kitchen to make them a cup of coffee.

"You don't need to use your cane," she hears Cassie say to Simon as she goes downstairs. "I'll help you."

Antonia is glad to leave Simon for a moment. She can't stop looking at his face. How sometimes he closes his eyes as if he doesn't know that sighted people keep their eyes open all the time unless they're asleep. How his eyes are a pale blue, yet his eyebrows and hair are dark. He's actually very attractive. Does he know it? What she really wants to find out is whether he's ever seen or if he's been blind from birth. At what stage in an acquaintance with a blind person can you ask that question, if ever? Do you have to wait for them to tell you?

In the sitting room, Cassie has spread a sheet of newspaper on the carpet and is placing her drawing pad and colouring pens on top of it. "I'm allowed to draw in here as long as I don't make a mess," she's explaining.

"I'm ashamed to say it," Antonia says, putting a tray on the coffee table, "but I used to get cross when Cassie drew. She'd sit drawing at the kitchen table and keep going over the edge of the paper onto the wood. I suppose I shouldn't tell you things like that. I mean, that I get cross. But, to be honest, now I love those marks all over the table as much as the pictures she draws."

"All parents get cross with their children at some point," says Simon. He's sitting on the floor beside Cassie. Antonia feels silly sitting above them in an armchair, but joining them on the floor would feel silly, too. As Simon gets up from the floor and gropes for the settee, she wonders whether sitting on the floor is easier for him. A simple descent to a hard, level surface.

"What support do you get," he says. "Does Cassie stay on for after-school care?"

"She won't stay," Antonia says. "She has tantrums if the other children go home and she's still there."

"Do you work?"

"I paint portraits, which means I can work from home. I do a lot of pet portraits," she laughs. "From photographs that I take."

"Fantastic," Simon says.

"But that all stops when I collect Cassie from school. I can't work once she's home. She somehow takes up all my attention."

"Do you mind if I ask where her father is?"

"He left when Cassie was a baby. When it was obvious she wasn't going to be your average child."

"Certainly not average."

Antonia nods in agreement, but then remembers he can't see her. "No," she says.

TWO DAYS LATER there's a letter from Simon North offering Cassie a place at his school. Within a couple of hours, he telephones and asks to meet with them again. He wants to tell them more about the school and arrange for her and Cassie to visit. He wants to talk to her about her doubts.

When they hang up, Antonia cannot recall ever mentioning her doubts. Dealing with blind people is, she decides, like dealing with mind-readers. Imagine a whole school of them, super beings with special powers. Did he hear it all in her voice? That she's scared she won't earn enough from portraits in York to support Cassie, that she feels guilty about moving away from her widowed mother, and that she's worried how long it will take Cassie to get to know a new house as well as she knows this one and what that might do to her confidence.

"YOU DON'T WANT CASSIE to have the stigma of going to a special school," Antonia's mother says. She's sitting at Antonia's kitchen table, rubbing at a felt-pen mark with her finger. "You want her to learn as much as children do at normal schools. If she's in a special school she'll sit around playing the tambourine and drawing pictures all day."

Antonia tries to prioritize her indignation. Should she defend her own profession first, or Simon's school which she hasn't seen yet, or Cassie herself?

"You're worried about the stigma? Cassie's as good as blind. She's going to need all the help she can get. That crappy little special needs unit she's in now just isn't up to it."

"You never know, the doctors might be able to do something."

"No, Mum. We do know. If anything, Cassie's eyesight is going to deteriorate altogether. There won't be any more blue-dark and black-dark for Cassie. There'll only be dark-dark."

Antonia rushes from the room so her mother won't see her tears.

By the time Simon arrives the following day, Antonia no longer has doubts. She has told her mother they are moving and, because her mother hates to drive, that she will be happy to pick her up from the railway station any time she wants to visit. And because she is her mother, and is entitled to her own opinions, Antonia and Cassie will drive back sometimes for visits.

When he comes, she lets Simon talk. They are in the kitchen this time, sitting at the table with mugs of coffee. The house is quiet because Cassie is at school.

"Antonia," Simon says, pausing.

"Yes?"

"I'm at a disadvantage here obviously because I can't see you, but I'm not sure you're listening to me, are you?"

"Yes. Well, I suppose no. I've already decided Cassie should go to your school."

"But you haven't seen it yet."

"True but, if this doesn't sound too insensitive, maybe seeing isn't everything."

Simon laughs. It's a deep, long laugh and Antonia can't stop herself giggling and then wonders why she's trying to stop herself. Her laugh dwindles only when she thinks how can Simon ever be attracted to a woman he can't see? Of course it's not only about looks but, really, how does a relationship with a blind person ever get going? Do you have to be courageous enough to say what your voice may have already revealed?

With Cassie, it's easy, they hug each other any time they like.

"If you don't mind, I mean, I don't want to offend you, but could you tell me something about what it's like for Cassie? And for you. Do you mind?"

Simon puts down his mug. "I can't tell you what it's like for Cassie. I had my sight until I was eighteen when I had a car accident. It's different for Cassie because she's had sight loss from birth. She lives in a different world from mine. Dreams, for example. How can I possibly know what goes on in her head when she dreams?"

"I'm sorry. I shouldn't have asked."

"No. You should have asked. You only want to understand what life is like for Cassie." He slides a flat hand along the edge of the table, stopping at the corner. "Faces," he says. "For a while after I lost my sight I remembered faces just as if I was looking at a photograph. But they began to fade and disintegrate. Voices have become the equivalent of faces, in a way." Simon starts to speak more quickly. "Sometimes I forget to smile because a smile is something shared, triggered by another person. Sometimes I close my eyes because there's no need for me to hold them open and my friends think I've fallen asleep when I'm actually paying great attention to them. I even get paranoid sometimes and imagine that people I know, friends even, are walking past and not bothering to say hello because they're in a rush or they don't like me any more because I'm such a drag. They think I'll never know so what does it matter."

Simon finds his coffee mug and takes a sip. Antonia is thinking about what he has said. She hopes Cassie doesn't start forgetting to smile.

"You know what would be a great thing to do? For Cassie, I mean," says Simon. "The next time it's windy or raining, wrap her up and take her outside. Get her to listen to all the different sounds. She'll know this but rain falling on grass sounds different from rain falling on stone. And the wind tells you how tall trees are, how big buildings are. Wind and rain make a two-dimensional world become three-dimensional."

"We'll both do it. My senses need developing, too. Perhaps not my sixth sense, though." She looks at her watch. "It's time to collect Cassie." She glances at him but his face is directed at the window, not at her. "Why don't you come with me? Cassie would love that."

"That would be great. You'll need to give me a hand, though. I have my cane but I'd like to hitch a ride on your elbow, if I may."

COMING BACK FROM SCHOOL, the pavement is wide enough for Cassie to walk between Simon and Antonia, holding both their hands. Antonia has collapsed Cassie's cane and put it in her handbag and Simon is using his cane to check for lamp-posts and where the edge of the pavement is. They should switch places really, so he is farthest from the traffic. She doesn't know if this is a suggestion she should make.

"That's a blackbird," Cassie says as they walk by trees. "There are some great tits and a blue tit. I think."

"We started learning together from tapes but her ears already have a much bigger vocabulary than mine," Antonia says.

"Mummy says we're moving to York, Simon. Is that where you live?"

"Yes, Cassie, it is."

"Do birds in York have a different accent from the ones here?"

"I don't know, Cassie." Simon smiles. "You can tell us when you get there."

Perhaps Birches

WHEN I LOOK AT IT THROUGH THE COLANDER, THE GARDEN looks smaller. The labels stuck to the window pane, however, look larger. One of these labels says "window" and the other says "garden," to denote what can be seen through the glass. As soon as she stuck the labels on, my daughter, Emma, realized this would be confusing and started to peel the "garden" label off, but I told her to leave it.

Yesterday, though, I started picking at the edges of both labels. I only stopped because I didn't like to see how baby-clean my fingernails are now that I'm not gardening. I don't need the labels — cooker, table, fridge, door — any more. My memory is as good as a post-aneurysmal, post-menopausal woman can hope for. The effect of a stroke on a body isn't unlike the effect of an earthquake on a city. Much can be restored, but you can't expect things to be exactly as they were.

If I take the labels off, Emma will think I'm being wilful. If I take them off, I'll have to explain to her that I remember everything now. But I might be wrong.

Putting the colander down, I wish my mind likewise held only solids. Things I can see and touch. Daughter, house, garden. I wish my mind would let the liquids, the intangibles, the invisibles, like grief and hurt and husband, drain away.

The other day, it's true, I forgot what the colander was for.

I had to check its name on the label Emma had stuck around the handle and look it up in the kitchen dictionary. Emma has put a dictionary in every room, even the study, though there's no point because I don't go in there. I removed the bathroom dictionary because I don't approve of books or magazines in bathrooms.

Emma has also put a notebook on the kitchen counter. I'm supposed to write my thoughts in it. When I first came home I did as I was told. But then my mind did become like a colander. Thoughts would slip through before I even got to the notebook. I swore a great deal, even though I know now that I never swear. Anger is terribly exhausting so I've stopped trying to write down what I'm thinking.

I SEE EMMA PARK HER FORD estate-something-or-other in the driveway. She doesn't look old enough to drive such a sensible car. In the kitchen, she unfurls a chart like a child just home from primary school. I smile and congratulate her. The chart is divided into boxes with a picture in each one and words underneath. It reminds me of something. I can't think what.

"Put it on the wall next to the dresser," I say.

"Wouldn't it be better, Mum, to put it between the cooker and the sink?"

"I don't want to splash water on it. It's so," I wait for the word to arrive, "pretty." I've learned that words can be like buses. None comes for ages and then they all come at once.

"It's not supposed to be pretty, it's supposed to help you. It should hang where you can easily see it."

I hold the chart where Emma wants it and watch my daughter yank off a bogey of Blu-Tack and roll it between two palms. When the chart is up we stand back to look. A movement through the window catches my eye. A pink-breasted bird — I'm sure I used to know its name — is on the grass. I pretend not to notice that the grass needs cutting.

"This is the wrong garden. There should be white stone and

water. Chalky, busy water."

"What do you mean?" Emma says.

I shake my head. "Never mind."

"Have you thought about doing some gardening? It would do you good. You used to be in the garden all the time. And," Emma hesitates, "it's getting so overgrown, it could do with some attention."

"No point now. It's autumn. Ah, I know. Periodical table."

"What?"

"That's what your chart reminds me of."

"It's the periodic table, not periodical."

"Right. Shall we have a coffee?"

"I'll make it," Emma says. "You sit down, read the paper. I've got a surprise for you." She looks at her watch.

"I've had enough surprises." I pick up the newspaper. I'm grateful that Emma brings it when she comes to see me every day after work. I haven't told her that by the time I've read to the end of a sentence I've forgotten how it started.

The doorbell rings. The surprise has arrived and I doubt it's a takeaway.

"I'll go," Emma calls.

I hear her shushing whoever it is at the door. There is more than one pair of feet in the hallway. A surprise visitor? Maybe Jennifer who I went to teaching college with, who is on my Christmas card list and who I haven't seen for years. Emma is too young to have learned that one sheds friends, even good ones, as inevitably as one sheds skin cells; it's part of the ageing process and perfectly natural. I certainly don't want to see anyone from my past when I don't know what my future holds.

Emma comes back into the kitchen. Behind her is Jocelyn. And Olivia. All the way from America. Isn't that a song? They must have been let out for bad behaviour. I push away my coffee and — my condition has its uses — remain seated. Jocelyn and Olivia sit, too, as if they wander into their mother's kitchen every day. They both need to tie their hair back.

"Mum," Jocelyn says, from the other side of the table. "I'm really sorry we couldn't get here before, you know, for Dad. We, well —"

"They had to wait to get permission to come," Emma interrupted.

Olivia glares at her. Emma shrugs.

"How are you feeling, Mum?" Jocelyn says. She's changing the subject. "You look great."

"You had to get permission to come?" I say it to Jocelyn. "Your father died and you had to get permission to come?"

"We're a community," Jocelyn says. "We have to seek the consent of every member of the circle. There's a process. Every decision must be a communal agreement. Autonomy is irresponsible and very destructive."

I raise my eyebrows. I can't help it.

"You wouldn't understand," Olivia says.

"You're right there," I say.

"How are you, Mum?" Jocelyn repeats. I am being managed, I can tell. She is using her training on me.

I'm half a bloody person, I want to shout. How can I look good? "I think you'd better go," I say instead.

Olivia smiles for the first time. It is not a kind smile. "Let's not fight Dad's war."

I lean on the table and stand up. I wouldn't tie their hair back, I'd cut it off. "I'd like you to go. It's not a war, it's a protest. It's all I have left."

"But it's not your protest. It never really was. You're confused. You've forgotten." Jocelyn moves round the table and I accept her hug. Jocelyn, middle-child, once pivot of the see-saw.

Jocelyn's hug tightens and it's this grip that releases me. I see Patrick holding the pole of a banner and I'm holding the other pole. Between us we're keeping the banner taut.

I jerk out of Jocelyn's grasp. "I want you to go. All of you."

The front door shuts behind them. Emma has gone, too,

which I suppose is what I asked for. I sit, head bowed. I can do this for hours. Closing my eyes, I see that garden again. Water lapping. I'm sitting on stone and it's making my bottom cold. I can see silvery aspens or perhaps they're birches.

THE TELEPHONE RINGS and, neck aching from awkward sleep, I follow the sound rather than try to remember where the telephone is.

"That was terrible."

"Emma, the situation is terrible."

"Your behaviour. I can't believe it. You've lost Dad —"

"I thought we'd all lost him."

"They're going back to America. They're very hurt."

"So hurt, you're the one telling me."

"They don't know I'm phoning."

"Of course they do."

"That's Dad speaking, not you."

When she says that, I can't speak, not for several moments. Not until the pain of missing him subsides.

"Do you remember a garden, Emma. A garden with aspens, or perhaps birches, and some water."

I wait for Emma to tell me to stop going on about a bloody garden.

"I can't, Mum," she says instead.

"Can't what?"

"I just can't."

She hangs up.

EMMA HASN'T COME with the paper for a couple of days, so I'm searching through old copies to see if I've missed any pictures. I'm cutting out the images I like best and gluing them in the notebook that I'm supposed to be writing in. A firefighter rowing a boat down a flooded road somewhere in Gloucestershire. A boy in Zimbabwe holding his mother's hand. Two footballers hugging. Reading whole sentences has got easier, but I find

I don't need to know what the stories are.

When I see a photograph of poor, sinking Venice I know I need to call Emma.

"Have I been to Venice?" I ask.

A pause. "Yes."

"Was there a garden in Venice?"

A longer pause. "Yes."

"Did I tell you much about it?"

"You didn't have to."

"What do you mean?"

"I was there."

"What?"

"I was there and it's all my fault."

Emma starts to sob. I hear the click of the phone as she hangs up. Again.

I'VE UPSET EMMA enough so there's only one place to find out about Venice. I haven't forgotten that the study is where we kept that sort of thing. But the study is where I last felt the warmth of Patrick's body. Before he left it behind along with his socks, towels, and spectacles, and everything else for me to tidy up.

I open the door and look only at the desk. I open a couple of drawers, remove a folder and turn to leave. Instead, I move toward my chair across the fireplace from his and sit down. The leather is corpse-cold and I stand up again. I put a hand on Patrick's chair and the leather is warm. I'll sit, for a few moments, just on the edge. But I'm leaning back, allowing myself to pretend the chair is Patrick. Expecting to cry, instead I breathe the deepest breath I've taken since he left me.

Inside the folder are tickets: plane, water taxi, Scuola Grande San Rocco, Palazzo Venier dei Leoni. A folded piece of Burano lace which smells of the sea. A menu from San Mark's we couldn't afford. A map which, to my eye, makes Venice look fish-shaped.

I look again at the Palazzo Venier dei Leoni tickets. Tickets to Peggy Guggenheim's unfinished home, which is where I remembered the garden. There's a stone seat and the three of us are sitting on it, Emma in the middle. We have a hangover from what Patrick is calling the Tintoretto terrors. Fifty-two paintings in one *scuola* and we looked dutifully at each one.

I point at a slender, headless woman by Giacometti and Patrick points at three slender birch trunks growing close together. "There you are," he says. "A natural Giacometti. The Three Graces, I'd call it. Maybe, we shouldn't bother with art and just appreciate nature more."

Emma sighs. "Do you mean artists shouldn't bother with art, or viewers should stop appreciating art?"

"Both," Patrick says. He winks at me.

Of course Emma sees.

"Why do you always do this?" Emma says. "Why does everyone have to think the way you think? For Christ's sake, Dad, try once in a while to see the other person's point of view."

"When did they talk to you?" Patrick says.

Emma, looking down at the gravel path, says nothing.

"I'm disappointed in you, Emma," says Patrick. "After all your mother and I have gone through, how can you take their side?"

"I'm not taking sides." A mutter.

"We're talking about the theft, the murder, of two young beautiful lives."

"You're being ridiculous." Emma's voice is rising. "They're not dead."

"You've lost both of your sisters to that cult, that evil machinery," Patrick says. "We've tried talking to them. Short of kidnapping them, all we can do is show them we object and hopefully, eventually, that will mean something to them."

"They've found their own way, that's all," Emma says. "It just doesn't happen to be the same way as yours."

"They've spoken to you, haven't they?" I keep my voice soft.

"They're always calling, emailing, telling me not to tell you. I'm sick to death of it."

I pull Emma toward me.

"I can't bear it, Mum," she says into my heart. "I'm stuck in the middle. They want you to leave that anti-cult group. It's causing problems for them."

"That's the bloody idea," Patrick says.

Emma pushes away from me. She stands and runs down the gravel path.

We let her go.

When we get back to the hotel we find a note from her telling us she's changed her flight and has gone straight home. She doesn't want to fly home with us the next day.

Three days later Emma and I watch as Patrick's dead body is carried from the study to the ambulance parked outside. She was the first person I phoned and she came immediately.

It's two o'clock in the morning and I wake up needing to go to the loo. It used to annoy me, this bellwether of old age, but I've begun to like moving around the house in the dark. I like to think of Olivia and Jocelyn at this time, too, wide awake in the California sunshine. I pretend they're playing volleyball on the beach or hiking in Yosemite.

Returning to my bedroom, I look out the window. In frail moonlight, I see movement, an almost-shadow, on the lawn; perhaps it's a fox. But the shape is human and it's heading round the side of the house. I rush to a front window and stand to the side, out of sight. The figure runs across the front lawn to a car parked on the road and opens the door. The light this activates is dim but the car looks like a Ford estate-something-or-other to me. The headlights go on and I am blind to detail. I watch the car leave.

As I get into bed I wonder if I should check all the doors and windows, but I know there's no need. A few sleepless minutes later, I get up again and go downstairs. Nothing seems changed. There isn't a new newspaper on the table or a new chart on the wall or any new food in the fridge.

I fetch a torch from the cupboard under the stairs and go outside. I'm too old to be scared of the dark, inside or out. The moonlight, in this black and white photograph world, reminds me to look up at the stars. I can't believe they're all supposed to be dead. To see them better, I turn off the torch and close my eyes to help them adjust. When I open my eyes again, I look at the garden, not up at the sky.

There's a shape near the end of the lawn which didn't used to be there. I go closer, long damp grass soaking my slippers.

Three tiny trees, freshly mulched. Planted in my garden.

Slender papery trunks silver in the moonlight.

Birches, I'm certain. Not aspens.

A natural Giacometti.

The Three Graces.

But how silly to plant them now, in autumn, the wrong time to plant anything. Anyone would know that.

If they're going to make it through winter, they're going to need looking after. To move them again would probably finish them off altogether.

I'll have to have a good look at them once it's light. Check my gardening books to see how to get them through to spring. Tomorrow I might even start clearing the rest of the garden. It's terribly overgrown. It's time to get earth underneath my fingernails again.

Travelling Light

THE WATER IN THE MARINA IS AS TAUT AS CELLOPHANE. SHE feels safe in the slow Mediterranean sunshine, but she wonders where she'll sleep tonight. Maybe on the beach with her backpack for a pillow; she's always wanted to do that. She's sitting on the jetty wall, rehearsing the lines she's prepared, when a man wearing ozone aftershave stops to talk to her. His name is Hugh, and even though she's disappointed that his English accent is the same as hers, she's glad when he offers to help. He's crewing too, he says; he's been taking boats from the Mediterranean to the West Indies and back for years. But, he's sorry to say, there's no room on his boat for her.

"I'm amazed," he says, sitting down on the wall beside her, "that your parents have let you do this. I mean, you look pretty young."

"Not that young. I'm eighteen." Hugh laughs and she notices that the tiny hairs on his temple are bleached even whiter than the hairs on his forearms. "Anyway," she adds, "There's no way they could have stopped me."

The truth, not that she'd admit it, is that they didn't even try.

As they walk along the pontoons together she notices how slowly the people on the boats move and how the sounds they make are dried up by the sun. Hugh calls out to the sailors he knows and she talks to the ones he doesn't. No one needs another pair of hands on their deck. Not until she asks a man who sounds Italian but doesn't look it because of his treacle-coloured hair. As soon as he's said he can take her, he starts lifting her backpack onto his boat, almost with her still inside its straps.

"Come," he laughs. "Plenty room. We are two. Aldo and Giorgio. From Italy. I am Aldo."

Standing on deck, she looks down at Hugh on the pontoon. She's not sure about the space Aldo has abruptly put between them.

THERE ARE TWO DAYS before they sail and she spends them mostly with Hugh. Like a million others, she tells him, she's taking a year out before university. Unlike a million others, she's going to sail, not fly. She wants to travel, not merely arrive. She's got a sister in Toronto she might visit, but only after she's been everywhere else.

Hugh tells her, just before he kisses her across a café table, that he loves the way her eyes gleam. "I'm twenty-four and I'm already jaded. Perhaps you can reinfect me with youthful optimism. Let me bathe in your aura."

"You can have my aura. I don't need it. I'm travelling light."

"Have you at least got room for this?" He takes out a pen and writes his email address on a paper napkin. "I'm crewing a flashy boat," he smiles. "I can get email any place, any time." When she's taken the napkin he adds, no longer smiling, "Look. Are you sure you can trust those guys, those Italians?"

"I can always jump ship." She smiles. "I'm a good swimmer."

SAILING AT LAST, she has to force herself to watch Hugh's waving figure on the end of the jetty rather than stare at the sleek horizon ahead. Aldo and Giorgio are sailing round the world. It will take a month just to cross the Atlantic. Aldo tells her she's climbed aboard his dream-coming-true. She can go all the way with them if she likes.

Before they have even left the Straits of Gibraltar, Aldo assigns her a non-nautical task.

"You teach me English," he says. It's not a question. "I teach English from music," he grins. "Coldplay."

"Learn, you mean. You learn English from music."

"Yes," nods Aldo as if that's what he said anyway. "You like Coldplay?"

Unfortunately — for it's a small boat — she doesn't.

Aldo says, "Coldplay is good. Is music about life. You do not understand. You are young."

NEARLY SEVENTY PER CENT of the planet is covered by water. She knew this but now she realizes what it means. She realizes, too, that sunrises and sunsets don't only happen in the east or west but in the entire sky. She reads the two novels she has with her twice and then starts on a collection of poetry. She'd worried that it was pretentious to have brought it with her but the poems sustain her far longer than the novels; it's like eating porridge instead of sugar puffs for breakfast. But even with her books she's running out of words to teach Aldo and Giorgio. They're tired of learning the anatomy of the boat in English and there's a limit to her nautical knowledge, anyway. They smile at each other instead of talking now. She isn't sure if she's bored of them, or of sailing, or both. She hadn't expected Italians to be dull.

On the afternoon of the fourteenth day, she's down in the cabin reading when Aldo shouts her up to the deck. A squall has exploded on the horizon and it's whirling their way. They clip themselves to the safety rail; they're safer out than in. The yacht tips steeply into the waves again and again, each time righting itself even though she thinks it can't. The rain is warm, the waves bigger than she's ever seen, bigger than she's ever imagined. The Italians yell with exhilaration and, laughing, she joins in. This is more like it; if only they could sail into a squall every day.

REACHING ANTIGUA on the other side of the Atlantic, they drop anchor in the harbour ready for the customs boat to come and check their passports. But they've been at sea for twenty-nine days; she can't wait any longer. She dives into the warm Caribbean Sea and swims to the shore where she grasps sand, exfoliating her palms under date palms.

That night, while she sways to a steel band on the beach, she decides she'll jump ship. She'll allow herself to fly on this next part of her journey. She's sailed across the Atlantic, after all, but she'll walk to the airport. She wants to smell tamarind and cinnamon trees, not see them through the smeared windows of a bus. The walk should take two days, she thinks, looking at the tourist map. Although she's not sure how fast she'll be in the heat, wrapped in an English skin, and with a backpack. Aldo and Giorgio say they're sorry she's leaving but they don't ask for her address when she goes.

BEFORE SHE STARTS HER WALK, she finds a telephone to ring her parents, proud that she's crossed an ocean. Her parents don't seem to realize what danger she could have been in, alone on a boat with two men — Italians — thousands of miles from land.

They tell her they haven't had a postcard from her yet, then add that the washing machine has broken down and they're having to buy a new one.

As she walks, few cars pass. Each one that does slows down to offer her a lift. She answers with a shake of her head. She wants to walk. At least that's what she wants until the evening, when she's burnt and tired and the centimetre of water left in her bottle is as warm as tea and she can't see anywhere close by in this deep green country to conceal her tent from the road. She's lost interest in looking for tree lizards and geckos. Now she's worried she might get too close to a racer snake and she wonders if the fruit bats bite.

So when a man named Jimmy stops, she's tempted to get

in and does. And when he invites her to stay the night in his house, she says she will.

JIMMY IS PROUD OF HIS HOUSE; he built it himself.

"I'll show you round," he says. "Follow me."

After the kitchen and the sitting room he opens the door to a bedroom so pink it looks like the inside of a mouth. He smiles and leads her up to a curvaceous dressing table with photographs on top. Pictures of a woman, blacker than he is. She looks closely.

"My wife," Jimmy says. "She's away right now. Isn't she cute?"

"Yes, she's very pretty."

Jimmy steps toward her. "Can I touch you?"

He is a big man but he moves quickly. Before she can answer he lifts his hand and touches her breast. His touch is gentle. She's a flower being picked by a giant.

She steps back, feels the bed against the backs of her knees.

"What about her?" She nods at the photographs.

"She won't mind," Jimmy says, but she's shaking her head, sliding sideways away from him.

He leaves the bedroom, lets her follow him out, and shows her the rest of the house. But she scarcely sleeps that night, watching the door handle of the spare room she's in, watching the window. She only knows she's safe in retrospect, when she's left Jimmy's house at dawn before he wakes, when she's walked three heavy miles and found a taxi, when she's in the airport lounge and a ticket to America is in her hand.

SHE LIKES THE PATTERN Miami makes from the air but at ground level its hot stench makes her queasy. She buys a map of America from a tourist information counter. She can't look at it as she sits on the bus to the Greyhound depot; it makes her feel sicker than the boat ever did. When she can look at it, there's Seattle on one side and New York on the other. *Frasier* and *Sex in the City*. Her eyes, her fingers, sweep from side to side. West coast. East coast. It's a while before she can focus on the states in between.

Kansas. Right in the middle. Dorothy and the Wizard of Oz.

The only non-fictional people she knows on this continent are her sister and her sister's family, there on a peninsula between two Great Lakes. A conversation with someone who knows her, a woman, would be more than nice.

She knows she's travelling, that this is what she wanted.

Yet for one hundred and fifty dollars she could be in Toronto within one day, seventeen hours and thirty-five minutes. Except there's a five-hour wait for the bus, during which she rings her sister's number seventeen times and each time there's no answer.

She can't ring her parents; they'll be in bed. There's no need to ring her parents, anyway; they know she's fine.

SHE HATES MIAMI but she loves America. She sits high up at the front of the bus as it glides down the freeway like a droplet of clean oil sliding down a can. Hour after hour. In Kentucky, her eyes can't look any more and she curls up dog-like on the seat with her sleeping bag over her. She wakes up in Detroit, changes buses, and sleeps again. She didn't know she was so tired.

Stepping down from the bus onto the ground in Toronto, her sandaled feet are freezing. Everything is freezing. She digs into her backpack and puts on socks, another t-shirt, a fleece and her thin rain jacket.

Her sister still isn't answering the phone but she finds the way to her house in the suburbs, three bus-rides away. No one is in. There's a light on next door so she crosses to their porch and pulls open the screen door, resisting the temptation to let it slam shut after she's knocked, the way they do in films.

"Next door?" says the neighbour. She won't tell this woman she's her sister. "She's on vacation — the whole family is. Gone up to the lakes. A friend's cottage, for the week. There's no phones. No cell phones work up there, either."

"Ah, well," she says. "I just called by on the off-chance." But her accent and her backpack are giving her away.

"You wanna come in? Get warm? Have some dinner with us?" says the neighbour. Her eyes are kind but curious.

"Oh no," she says. "Thanks, I'm fine. I'd better be going."

She walks as fast as she can with the backpack to the bus stop; at least it warms her up.

When the next bus comes, the driver tells her the airport is only two buses away. Sitting on the bus, she swallows her travel sickness and takes out her map of America. Each state looks like a piece in a jigsaw that someone has already put together.

At the airport, she finds an empty row of seats and sits with the map on her knees. She hasn't bought a ticket anywhere yet and it's gone eleven at night. She buys a Coke and a muffin and carries on looking at the map. However long she stares, it remains jigsaw-flat. A woman comes over and sits in a seat nearby, catches her eye and smiles. She doesn't want to talk to anyone; she's tired of meeting people. Across the concourse there's a row of phones. She should have rung her parents when she was in Miami after all. They'd have known her sister was away; they always know more about her sister's life than hers.

She's never travelled a thousand miles by mistake before.

Next to the row of phones across the concourse there's an internet café. She could look on the web to help her decide. Grand Canyon. Golden Gate Bridge. Teotihuacan pyramids. Or she could send an email. Have at least half a conversation with someone she knows.

She starts searching for the napkin that Hugh wrote his address on. She looks in the bag where she keeps her money and passport. It's not in there. She checks all the pockets of her backpack. It isn't there, either. She bends over her backpack and takes everything out, placing it on the floor until it surrounds her like flotsam. The woman sitting nearby is looking at her, and so are other people. She doesn't care. They don't know what it's like to live out of a backpack, to have nowhere private to do things and anyway it's cleaner out here than in the washrooms.

She checks the pockets of the shorts she was wearing at the time, even though she's washed them at least twice since. She slides her hand around the bottom of the empty backpack. She turns over every page of the book of poems. It isn't there. Maybe it's in one of the novels she left on the boat for Aldo and Giorgio to read. Or perhaps she chucked it out, in the days when she'd believed it was better to travel light.

The Triskelion Necklace

CYCLING DOWN TOWN CROSS AVENUE IN THE DARK, LAURA Gray tried to imagine being locked in a tiny room for seven years. It was almost half her life. Fitting that amount of time into her mind was like trying to fold up a pane of glass. Yet seven years was how long an American called Terry Anderson had been kidnapped for, according to the papers she was delivering this morning. All because Hezbollah Shiite Muslims didn't like Americans. She didn't know what Hezbollah Shiite Muslims were. She would look them up in her encyclopaedia when she got home.

Laura stabbed her handlebars into the hedge that smelt of cat pee and opened number thirty-one's gate. Walking up the path, she folded the newspaper into thirds and squeezed until it cracked, which was the only way to make it fit through a letter-box designed for a dolls' house. The Hezbollah Shiite Muslims had shoved Terry Anderson into a car boot while he was dropping off his friend after a game of tennis. Or had pushed him into the back seat of a car, depending which paper you read. He was still wearing his tennis clothes. He hadn't even had a shower.

It was a longer ride to the final house on her paper round. As she pedalled, she tried to imagine breathing the dry air of a prison cell in Lebanon but she couldn't because she lived in bloody Bognor where the air was always damp. The people who had kept Terry Anderson prisoner had brought him new shoes, a white shirt, and a cardigan the night before they released him, but they hadn't mended his glasses. In the photographs you could see that one of the plastic arms that curled over his ears was missing. His face was very pale, like the underside of woodlice.

Laura freewheeled into the driveway of the last house.

"About bloody time." A man in a suit was standing by the open door of a sports car. Arm out, palm up. "You're supposed to deliver the papers, not read them."

"Sorry," Laura said, clenching her brakes. She didn't stop close enough to hand him his Daily Express so she waddled forward, straddling the crossbar. As she moved, the handlebars tipped to one side, pulling the bicycle over.

"Ow." The crossbar bashed her knee and she dropped the paper.

The man bent to snatch it up. "Don't hold your breath for a Christmas tip," he said as he got into his car.

She watched him reverse onto the road without checking for traffic. Driveway roulette. Not a game Terry Anderson would play. She stood cupping her knee with her hand. As she mounted her bicycle, the house's security light switched on. She wasn't crying; it was the brightness of the light that made her eyes water.

LAURA CYCLED TO THE NEWSAGENT's shop on the way home after school. Cathy was over by the boxes of crisps that had holes in their sides as if someone desperate for monosodium glutamate had punched their way in. With Cathy, as always, was Sonia. Laura had to share a locker with Sonia because their surnames were alphabetical neighbours. Teachers had no imaginations.

Laura passed the money to the shop assistant. She would buy her own newspaper from now on rather than read them on her paper round. She would choose a different paper each day, though not the ones with naked women in them. The same sort of women were on the covers of the magazines behind the shop assistant. It was hard to stop your eyes rising to those vast shiny breasts floating on the top shelves like helium balloons.

As Laura held out her hand for her change, she felt a nudge and lurched.

"Sorry." Cathy smiled as she watched Laura bend to retrieve coins. Cathy picked up Laura's paper and flipped through the pages.

"Fascinating," Cathy said. "Riveting stuff."

When Laura stood up, Cathy slapped the paper shut and dropped it back on the counter. Laura pushed the messy bundle deep into her school bag and left the shop. Cathy wouldn't understand the pleasure of opening a smooth, flat newspaper or the way it puffed up as you turned the pages as if you were breathing life into it.

"You're back early," Laura's mother said as she turned away from the sink, sleeves pushed up over the nubs of her wrinkled elbows.

"I'm late, if anything."

Her mother blinked, not just with her eyelids like normal people; she scrunched her eyes up until they disappeared.

"I don't know why you bothered getting that." Her mother pointed to the paper Laura was taking out of her bag. "Dad'll be home with his soon. It's just extra clutter." She gave her head a small shake and her auburn perm quivered.

"I'd rather have a paper that's got actual news in it, instead of just photos of people on telly. That's why it's called a newspaper."

Lisa, Laura's little sister, came into the kitchen. "What's going on?" she asked.

"Nothing," Laura said, passing her on her way into the hall.

"That's the whole bloody point."

THE NEXT MORNING, when she had finished her paper round, Laura cycled down to the seafront as usual. She rested her bicycle against the railings where she could see it and jumped down to the shingle. The sea was mostly grey today with greenish tinges in its crinkles like moss on a corrugated iron roof. The best thing about living in this town was being able to come to the edge of the land. The end of England. Sliding her eyes along the horizon, she felt instantly calm. She took the longest, deepest breath that she could. People with asthma must feel something like this when they sucked their inhalers. Sometimes in French Laura watched Colin Gibson grab the pale blue contraption from his pocket and breathe in with a sleepy baby look. It reminded her of when Lisa used to suck her thumb. She'd made sure Lisa grew out of that habit. You definitely didn't want to still be a thumb-sucker when you started school. At school, you shouldn't do anything that made you stand out. You shouldn't come first in exams. You shouldn't prefer watching the news to watching *Coronation Street*. You shouldn't forget to try to make friends with people, even if you didn't know what to say to them.

A gull rose from behind a mound of pebbles, close enough for her to see the perfect black circle of its pupil surrounded by a Polo mint of yellowish-green, so pale it was a colour she couldn't name. There was a red patch near the end of its beak, perhaps a fish-blood stain. She watched the bird turn into a silhouette then dissolve into brightness.

"THERE YOU GO." Laura's mother put a fourth plate of bangers, beans, and mash on a fourth tray. Laura lifted the gold handles of her tray and took it into the lounge. She hated her tray, how some of the fake gold had worn off the handles to expose white plastic underneath. Normal families didn't eat off trays in front of the telly; they ate sitting round a table talking to each other.

Laura stabbed a sausage with her fork and the tray tipped. The plate slipped but not far because of the tea towel her mother always folded onto each of their trays. Laura always got Sussex windmills. She lifted the entire impaled sausage to her mouth with the fork and bit the end off. Then she twisted the fork and bit off the other end. No one said anything. They were all watching *East Enders*. She started reading the newspaper she'd placed on the sofa beside her. She knew the Maastricht Treaty was going to create a European Union but she didn't know what that actually meant. She turned the page to find something she could understand.

"What are you reading about?" her father said, smiling in his armchair, the magnification of his glasses making his eyes even softer than they really were.

Laura glanced at her mother. Her mother never shushed them. She didn't even frown when they talked over one of her soaps; she just kept staring at the telly as if she couldn't hear them.

"Auras," lied Laura, thinking of an article she'd read earlier that evening. She didn't want to find out that her father knew even less about Maastricht than she did. "It's not proper news," she said. "I don't know why I'm reading it really."

"Nice," her father said. He nodded and looked back at the telly.

If her mother hadn't been there, if the telly hadn't been on, Laura would have told her father she'd looked up the word aura. That was why she'd left the lounge before tea. And, if they'd been having a conversation, he'd have said that was clever, to know to look words up and remember what they meant and what had it said auras were exactly? They were energy fields around your body, she would have said, and they were the colours of the rainbow.

Laura looked at her family to see what colours their auras were. Her father's was yellow. Easy. Lisa's was orange. Nearly as easy. She couldn't tell what colour her mother's aura was.

She realized that was because it was colourless, see-through. If her mother knew this, she would dye it to try to make herself more interesting, like she dyed her hair, but after a bit it would fade and become transparent again. Her mother was like the steam coming out of a kettle. Hot enough to hurt but gone the next minute. Her father was always solid, visible, yellow like the sun you knew was there even when it was cloudy, even at night when it was on the other side of the planet. You could walk behind his tallness, his broad hips and breadloaf shoulders, and not be afraid that there was no back to him. Her mother was like television. The picture was only on the front. Sometimes you would hover your palm close to the screen to feel the prickle of static but when you put your hand flat on the screen all you felt was cold glass.

LAURA WAS SUPPOSED to be doing her history homework but she couldn't stop looking at the photographs in the Sunday magazine lying open on her bed. Triangles of cloudless blue sky were slotted between pyramid-shaped mountains. The lakes were as shiny as mirrors. Not a street or a town or a city or a person for miles. Now and again she picked it up to sniff the paper. The chemical smell was delicious.

The article was mostly pictures. British Columbia was a strange name but it was in Canada and Canada used to belong to Great Britain so that must be why. Yet British Columbia looked nothing like Britain. There was an address at the end of the article to write to for a holiday brochure. The address was in Victoria which Laura thought was in Australia but when she checked her atlas she saw that Canada had one, too, at the bottom of a large island that looked as if it was trying to nose its way into America.

She'd better finish her homework. She closed the magazine and put it on top of a pile of newspapers on the floor between her bed and the window. The pile was getting high but it didn't seem right to throw away all those important things that had happened to people, all those things that were still happening. Keeping each newspaper and magazine seemed more respectful. And there was so much information in them. There was so much she didn't know, so many things going on in places she hadn't known existed.

THE DRIVEWAY ROULETTE MAN was true to his word; he didn't give Laura a Christmas tip. The people with the tiny letterbox did, however, so she was more gentle with their *Daily Mail* after that. Fourteen other houses on her paper round gave her a tip as well, even though hardly any of them had ever met her. One woman, who always opened the door and said hello as Laura handed her the paper, gave her a torch she could wear on her head. It was perfect when the street lights were too dim for her to read the house numbers pencilled on the top edge of each newspaper. She'd never had a present from someone she didn't know before.

Her favourite Christmas present, though, was the necklace. It was real silver.

"It's a Celtic design," her father said as she unwrapped it. "Happy Christmas, love."

Lisa kneed across the carpet to look.

"It's called a triskelion," her father added. "It means three-legged in Greek."

Laura stood to kiss her father and then went over to her mother to kiss her, too. As she sat back down, her mother was smiling and looking toward her but not quite as far as her. It was as though her eyes were stuck on their telly-viewing setting, even though it was switched off while they were opening presents.

"It doesn't really have three legs," Laura said. "They're more like linked spirals, like waves about to break."

`That's a nice way of looking at it," her father said. "A triskelion represents things that come in threes," he explained. "Like body, mind, and spirit. Land, sea, sky. Past, present, future."

"Lift your hair." Lisa knelt behind Laura and fastened the chain around her neck.

Laura dropped her hair then smoothed it down with the palms of her hands. "How do you know about triskelions?"

Don't encourage him," groaned her mother.

Laura looked at her father but he looked away before she could catch his eye.

Her mother never wanted any of them encouraged, not her father, not Lisa, not her.

"Why don't we have Christmas dinner at the table this year?" Laura said. "We could bring the kitchen table in here. There would be lots of room."

"That's just like you to come up with such a good idea," her father said.

"I've got a nice candle," Lisa said. "And we've got those new serviettes we've never used."

"Let's do it," their father said. "Let's do it now."

Laura stood and left the lounge before her mother could object. Lisa and her father came, too.

Lisa and Laura took one end of the table, and, with their father at the other end, they managed to work out a way to angle it so they could get it into the hall. Laura and Lisa giggled when one of the legs tapped the frosted glass in the kitchen door.

Their mother was still sitting in the lounge when they brought the table in and set it down. She blinked her eyes hard and stood up. Laura followed her back into the kitchen.

While her mother got peas out of the freezer, Laura turned on the radio. She twisted the dial away from Radio Two which was playing "Santa Claus is coming to Town" and kept twisting until she came across Handel's *Messiah*. "That's better," she said.

"What are you doing?" her mother said. "Put it back to something we can sing along to."

Laura ignored her and started getting the cutlery out of the drawer to take into the lounge. Her mother didn't change it back to Radio Two, though.

Laura realized as she cleaned her teeth that night that moving the table — and laying out the cutlery and finding serviettes and putting Lisa's candle in the middle — had been the Christmassy family moment she'd been trying to create, and it had come and gone without her paying enough attention. Once the table had been in the middle of the lounge, with the armchairs and even the telly pushed back, they had all just sat there without saying anything except mmmm and delicious and that was only her father. Even Lisa couldn't think of anything to say.

And tomorrow it would be back to tea on a tray in front of the telly, with windmills under your plate to stop it sliding. Maybe it was just as well.

One thing had happened, though. She had found out her father knew about Celtic mythology; she didn't think he knew about anything except the fridges at the factory where he worked. She would ask him more about it tomorrow. She would ask just out of curiosity, not because she believed in signs or symbols because she didn't; she was an atheist.

The Christmas holiday was over. After her paper round on the first day of term, Laura cycled down to look at the sea. She left her bicycle in the usual spot and ran across the shingle to the sand exposed by the low tide. She was wearing her old trainers so it didn't matter if she was walking on the salty sand. The sun was up, although it was too cloudy to be able to tell where it was. Laura wished she didn't have to go to school. She hated the first day back. Everyone would be busy catching up with each other after the holidays and it would be even more obvious that she didn't have any friends.

She put a hand on top of a post moist with bright green seamoss and lifted a foot onto the groyne, testing it for skiddiness. Jumping down to the other side, she saw a dark shape lying where the waves soaked into the sand. She walked toward it.

It was a whale, or a shark. Dead. Broken. Snapped in the middle. Or maybe not snapped. Its long, sharp tail, almost as long as its body, was high in the air. The creature was moving, but only just. The poor thing looked so uncomfortable, its fins pointing at different angles like a person with all four limbs broken. She went closer, cold sea water seeping through her trainers.

Its broad mouth was gummy and its teeth were spiny. Laura crouched by the head end and looked into one of its eyes. A glistening darkness that was solid, like the opposite of outer space. You could tell what an animal like a cat or a dog was looking at, but this creature seemed to use its eyes to absorb rather than to see. The tail stopped moving. The creature was dying in front of her, craving salty water and the constant rhythm of the sea. The water it was lying in was too shallow and the tide was still going out.

Laura touched the triskelion around her neck, tracing the shape of three waves about to break. She moved closer, feeling like a crab as she stayed in a crouch.

"It's okay, I won't hurt you." She tried to speak soothingly; a whale would never have heard a human voice before. She moved closer and reached out her hand. She had to be careful to avoid the gashes in case they were gills. That would be like poking someone in the eye. The skin was rough like sandpaper. She moved her fingers in the other direction. Smooth. Like snake skin, you had to know which way to stroke. The eye remained dark and blank and cosmic and the mouth didn't move.

Laura stood up. She couldn't see anyone on the beach or any cars on the road along the prom. She ran as fast as she could toward the shingle, gasping and jerking each time the sand changed invisibly from soft to hard. The shingle was even more difficult to run on, but she got to her bicycle as quickly as she could. There was a phone box by the pier. She pedalled faster than she ever had before, but it didn't hurt like it did running the one hundred metres at school.

When she reached the phone box she braked so hard she nearly went over the handle bars. She leant her bike against the red paint and winced as it crashed to the ground. Never mind.

Did she have any money on her? Yes, her purse was in her anorak pocket. Should she dial 999? You didn't even need money for that.

She yanked open the heavy door and stepped into the phone box. It stank of urine. She hoped the phone hadn't been vandalized.

Thank goodness. There was a dial tone.

"I've found something on the beach," she said quickly when a woman answered. "I shouldn't have phoned 999 probably but it's a whale or a shark or something."

"All right, love," said the woman. She didn't sound cross. "I'll put you through to the local police station."

"I found a whale on the beach. Or it might be a shark," she said as soon as the call was answered. "Three groynes along from the pier, towards Selsey," she added. "On the sand."

"Righty-ho," said a male voice. "You hang on there. We'll send someone along."

"Thank you," she said before she hung up. She meant thank you for listening to me, thank you for caring about the creature, thank you for taking me seriously.

Before Laura made her next call, she swallowed. There was salt in her saliva, as if she'd been swimming in the sea. She pushed a coin into the slot and dialled.

"Mum, it's me."

"Laura, where are you? You'll be late for school."

"I found a shark, Mum, on the beach. Or a whale. It's still alive."

"Don't go anywhere near it."

"It's stuck, Mum. Stranded."

"Someone else will see it and do something. Animals can

take care of themselves. You come home."

"I phoned the police."

"Oh."

Laura could hear muttering.

"It's Dad. You all right?"

"I found a shark on the beach. Still alive. Just. It's big. Three times as long as me."

"Amazing. And you've called for help?"

"I phoned the police."

"Good girl. Where are you?" her father said. "A shark, I can't believe it. I'll come and get you. What?" He was talking to her mother now. "Yes, I darn well do need to see it."

WALKING ALONG THE CORRIDOR to maths that afternoon, Victoria came up beside her. Victoria was one of those people who always had someone to talk to at lunchtimes. Her aura was orange like Lisa's.

"You're not wearing that necklace," Victoria said. "I was looking at it in English this morning. It's really pretty."

A silver necklace would go very well with Victoria's pale blue eyes, wheat field hair, and accessory freckles.

Laura put her hand to her throat. "It disappeared from my locker."

"You share with Sonia, don't you?" Victoria said.

"I do."

"Bitches," Victoria said. Everyone knew about Cathy and Sonia.

"I shouldn't have worn it on a hockey day. I thought it would be safer in the locker than in the changing rooms."

"Poor Marie has to share a locker with Cathy," Antonia said. "I call Cathy and Sonia the locker louts."

Laura laughed. "Good one."

As they turned into the maths room, Victoria mumbled, "God, I hate this place."

AT THE LIBRARY AFTER SCHOOL, Laura found all the books with shark and whale pictures in them and piled them up on a table in front of her. There it was. The torpedo body with a long bent tail. Not a whale. A thresher shark with a big harvesting tail like a scythe. Possibly one of three species: bigeye, pelagic, and common. She thought it was a common, because it had a white tummy and because it had been in the English Channel.

When she got home her father told her he'd been on to the council and the police and it was a thresher shark and there were three messages. Two from the local newspaper and one from the television station in Southampton. That evening, two reporters came, one with a camera round her neck and another with a big camera on his shoulder. They interviewed her in the lounge because it was too dark for the beach, they said. Her mother sat in her armchair with the newspaper on her lap and didn't say anything about missing her soaps.

It was weird, seeing herself in the newspaper, more weird than seeing herself on telly because that was just an image that came and went, especially as her father managed to mess up the video recording and taped some program about battleships instead, which was actually quite interesting. Now she was one of the people in the piles of newspapers on her bedroom floor. Now she was someone that things happened to.

"HI BRUCE," Cathy said, two days later as Laura approached the lockers. People turned to see who Cathy was talking to.

"Duh-da, duh-da." Sonia made *Jaws* film soundtrack noises and placed her thumb against her forehead so her hand stuck up over her head like a fin, sort of. Laura stood waiting for her turn at the locker. She couldn't blame anyone for laughing, it was almost funny; she just wished she understood the reference to Bruce. She also wished she'd had a chance to see the shark one more time, but that was a selfish thing to think. It was brilliant that the people from Greenpeace had gone to the beach and waited for the tide to come in then helped the shark back out to sea. One of the pictures in the paper had been two-thirds filled up with grey sea with a tiny black dot near the horizon. The caption said the dot was the shark, but really it could have been anything.

Sonia shut and locked the door before she stepped back from the locker, so Laura had to get out her key to open it again. She pictured the black dot disappearing altogether, free to go wherever it wanted.

"I wanted to pass on my condolences, Brucie," Cathy said. "I hear your little shark got washed up in Newhaven yesterday. Dead as a doornail."

Laura closed her eyes briefly, left the locker door open, and started to walk away.

"Oh, no you don't," Cathy said. She flung out her hand and grabbed Laura's hair.

BY THE END OF THE LESSON, Laura was struggling to concentrate on what the maths teacher was saying, which was annoying because she liked maths. In maths, however difficult the questions were, you knew there was an answer that you could work out if you tried.

"You all right?" Victoria said, coming up beside her as they left the classroom. "You look a bit pale."

"Had a bit of a run in with the locker louts." Before she could stop herself, she reached her hand towards her head.

"What did they do?" Laura flinched as Victoria gently lifted a strand of her hair. "God. Come on." Victoria slipped her fingers under Laura's arm. "Sod it if we're late for French."

She took Laura to the nearest toilets and got her to sit on a loo with the lid down so she could look at her scalp properly. "I'm taking you to the nurse," she said.

"No." Laura's peripheral vision shrank and the air was speckled like sand. She felt herself swing sideways.

"Head between your knees," Victoria said, putting her hand

on the back of Laura's neck and guiding her down.

"I can't go to the nurse," Laura said, as the sand disappeared from her vision.

"Laura, you can't let them get away with this."

"But they'll beat me up even more next time if I tell on them."

"Okay. We'll go to the nurse and say you feel ill because of your period and you have to go home."

Victoria started to arrange strands of Laura's hair over the cut in her scalp. "Put your hands just below your tummy-button when we get to the nurse's office."

LAURA CAME THROUGH the back door. Her father was sitting at the table in the kitchen.

"Dad? What are you doing home?" Laura put her bag down and went over to kiss his cheek.

"All right, love?"

The back door opened and her mother came in with two Tesco shopping bags. "Oh," said her mother, blinking. "Why are you both home?"

Laura began to feel prickly all over her body, even under her fingernails. She pulled out the chair opposite her father and sat down. She couldn't lift her ribs high enough to get the air she needed. She bent over and put her head between her knees like Victoria had told her to do.

"What's the matter?" her mother asked.

"My hair got pulled." Laura lifted her face out of the bowl of her skirt.

"Let's have a look." Her mother's fingers as they parted her hair were almost gentle.

"Things got a bit energetic in netball."

"Nasty. Look at this, Brian," her mother said.

"What happened, love?" her father said. He reached across the table to hold Laura's hand but didn't get up to see.

"Got my hair tangled in an earring."

"They shouldn't be allowed to wear earrings," her mother said.

"They're not," Laura said.

"I should ring the headmaster."

"Head teacher."

"I should."

"Don't worry about it, Mum."

"Only if you're sure."

"I'm sure."

"Dad collected you from school, did he?"

"No, he was here when I got in."

It didn't seem interesting any more that she'd been sent home in a taxi and that Victoria had stayed with her right up until she closed the car door.

"Dad," Laura said. His big shoulders looked soft, filleted. "Why are you home?"

"What's going on?" Her mother looked around as if she was in someone else's kitchen. "We need more chairs in here."

Laura stood up and her mother sat down. "For heaven's sake, Brian, what is it?"

Her father took a deep breath but didn't say anything.

"What's happened, Dad?"

He breathed deeply again. "I've lost my job," he said as he exhaled. "Twenty-two bloody years."

"What do you mean, you've lost your job?" said Laura's mother. Her voice sounded thin, like bubblegum about to pop.

"Looks like they got a bit tired of my ideas. Well, I call them ideas. They call them complaints."

What a relief. Lisa wasn't dead. Her father wasn't dying.

"It's okay, Dad. You can get another job. I thought it was something much worse."

"Much worse? How much worse?" Her mother was almost shouting. "We've got to put food in your mouths, clothes on your backs. There's a recession on if you hadn't noticed."

"It's not that easy, love." Laura's father looked at her with his kind, magnified eyes.

Laura's scalp was aching. The prickling had come back. She put both palms flat on the table. The coolness helped.

"I told them not to buy that new equipment, but did they listen to me?" Her father sighed. "They've got themselves in a real pickle now."

"I'm not going to work," Laura's mother said. She stood up and walked over to the counter. Laura thought about sitting down in the chair again but she was afraid the movement would make her sick. Her mother picked up the kettle and started to fill it with water.

"You might have to, love. We've got to be realistic."

"No!" her mother shouted, making Laura jump. She thumped the kettle onto the counter and flipped round to face Laura's father. Water flowed into the kitchen sink. "I am not getting a job. I'm already a servant as it is, looking after the three of you." She turned back to the sink and carried on filling the kettle.

Laura looked at her father. He didn't look as surprised as she expected. He tipped his face into his hands. Her mother stayed at the sink. She'd filled the kettle and turned off the tap but she hadn't plugged the kettle in. She just stood there looking out the window at two starlings eating the seeds on the bird table. Her mother hated starlings. She was always saying they carried diseases. She didn't say anything this time; she just seemed to be watching them. Her broad back and her rounded hips looked solid, not like flesh at all, as if she were a waxwork at Madame Tussaud's. If you touched her, you wouldn't be able to stop yourself crying out in surprise at the hardness where softness should be.

THE SATURDAY NEWSPAPERS had articles about an American called Jeffrey Dahmer who had been sentenced to nine-hundred and fifty-seven years in prison for killing fifteen people, all men. The worst part was a boy who two women had found wandering naked in a street. The women had called the police but the police had believed Jeffrey Dahmer when he said the boy was his boyfriend. They had let him take the boy away.

Jeffrey Dahmer kept the boy's skull as a souvenir.

Sometimes Laura imagined the shark was still alive. Its cosmic eyes were leading it out of the murky English Channel, a torpedo through the grey Atlantic Ocean. It was leaping over the locks in the Panama Canal and up through the blue Pacific all the way to the mountainous coast of British Columbia. It would be too cold to go the other way round, through the icy Northwest Passage.

Sometimes, as it swam, the shark would shoot up into the air and balance for a tiny moment with its tail on the surface of the sea. Then it would dive back down into the Caribbean indigo, never again landing on hard sand.

There was a knock on Laura's bedroom door.

"It's me," Victoria said, angling her head around the door. "Can I come in?"

"Of course." Laura put the newspaper down on her desk. "I heard the doorbell but I didn't think it would be for me." She shouldn't have said that. Then again, it was no secret she didn't have any friends.

"How did you know where I live?"

"Taxi, der-brain." Victoria went toward the bed as if to sit down but stopped halfway. "Shit, what are all these newspapers?"

Victoria stood staring at the nine piles of newspapers stacked against the wall. Eight of them were waist high; the ninth was up to Laura's knees. Victoria went over to the nearest pile and laid her hand on top. "Why on earth do you have so many newspapers? Are you nicking them from your paper round?" It was a joke, but neither of them laughed.

"There's just so much information in them that it's hard to get rid of them." Laura wouldn't mention to Victoria how she liked the inky smell of them or the way the newspapers made her bedroom sound less empty, as if there were other people in the room with her.

Victoria sat down on the bed but kept looking at the piles rather than at Laura. "So you get a paper every day?"

"Well, more than one most days. I started off buying just one but they all have different articles in them and even when they're on the same subjects they're written in a different way and include different things. If I buy two or three I can compare them. It's interesting. Journalists aren't as objective as you think. They decide what to say and what not to say. They can twist things."

"You sound like my dad," Victoria said. "He's always ranting about the media." Victoria looked at Laura. "You can see this is pretty weird, can't you? They're filling up your bedroom."

Laura liked the way she could reach out and touch the nearest piles as she lay in bed. However chilly her bedroom was, the papers always felt warm. She didn't know why that was.

"Trust me, this is weird." Victoria said. "You've got to chuck them out. All of them. Buy an encyclopaedia."

"I've got an encyclopaedia," Laura said, pointing to her bookcase. "But this is current affairs, what's going on now. It's important to know what's happening."

"It's good to keep up with the news, but this isn't normal."

Laura tried to explain. "There's so much going on in the world that's wrong. Wars. Murder. Famine. It's awful. I'm trying to understand it so maybe I can do something about it when I leave school."

"You won't be able to get out of your room if you keep going at this rate." Victoria laughed, but Laura knew she was serious. "You know there are people who can't throw anything away? Not even their rubbish. It's disgusting." Victoria shuddered and folded her arms. "Their houses get fuller and fuller until they get stuck inside and die. It's horrible. I'm not making this up. It's a disease. My sister told me. She tells me every time I leave my room in a mess. One man ended up making tunnels in all the rubbish so he could get from his bed to the sink for water. Every room was completely filled with stuff. He had three cats and they all died."

Laura hadn't read about that in any of her newspapers. "I'm not like that." She went over to the bed to sit next to Victoria. She knew Victoria was going to leave now and would never be her friend. There was nothing she could do about it.

"This sounds stupid," Laura admitted, because it didn't matter what she said now, "but it feels disrespectful to throw away all these people's lives."

They sat side by side on the bed.

"It's not stupid." Victoria sighed. "But it is weird."

Laura nodded. "I know."

They both laughed at the same time.

Victoria curled her hair behind her ears. It made her ears stick out, although Laura didn't tell her that. "Don't you want to do something to help the world?" Laura said. It was the biggest question she could think of. She'd never said it to anyone. She was scared of asking it, because if the answer was no, then she wouldn't be able ever to have a conversation with that person again. They wouldn't be able to understand each other; it would be like listening to a Japanese radio station.

"Of course I do. Everyone does."

Laura wasn't sure about that.

"You can make a difference and you will, I know you will," Victoria said. "But you can't solve all the world's problems and you can't keep all these papers."

Laura looked over at the stacks of newspapers with a feeling of panic.

"I'm surprised your mum and dad haven't already told you to chuck them out," Victoria said.

They hadn't said anything, but then again they had other things on their minds. Her mother must come into her room sometimes because she hoovered. Laura noticed the brush lines in the carpet. She imagined her mother vacuuming around the piles of newspapers, too busy thinking about what had happened last night in *Coronation Street* to wonder about the growing stacks in her daughter's room. Laura had seen her father glance at the piles. He'd raised his eyebrows once or twice when he'd popped his head around the door to say hello, but he'd never said anything.

"My dad lost his job," Laura said.

"That's shitty," Victoria said. "There are so many redundancies at the moment. My mum and dad are glad they're teachers. It's hard to get rid of teachers."

"That's the problem," Laura said. "My dad wasn't made redundant, he was sacked. So there's no redundancy pay. No lump sum. Nothing."

"Oh," Victoria said. "My mum's friend got ten thousand pounds. Or was it twenty. I never remember numbers. A lot, anyway."

"I could just keep one week's worth at a time," Laura said, looking at the papers.

Victoria nodded. "Good idea. Let's get rid of all of them except the last week."

Laura went over to the pile nearest her bed. She picked up the magazine with British Columbia on the front and held it up for Victoria to see. "I'm keeping this one."

"Wow, where's that?" Victoria reached for the magazine.

"Canada. British Columbia."

"We should go there one day. Can I borrow it?"

Laura wanted to say no, but remembered you had to make an effort if you wanted to have friends. She handed it to Victoria.

"Thanks." Victoria rolled the magazine up into a tube. Laura tried not to wince when Victoria drummed her knees with it.

"By the way," Victoria added, "it's the name of the mechanical model, the fake shark they used in Jaws."

"What is?"

"Bruce."

"Did you know that?" Laura asked.

"Of course not. I told my sister and she worked it out."

"It's good," Laura said. "You've got to give them that."

Victoria dropped the magazine on the bed where it stayed in a curl. One of the corners was bent. She stood and picked up a stack of newspapers. "Get some plastic bags," she said. "Lots of them."

WHEN LAURA GOT HOME from school on Monday, her father's CV was lying on the kitchen table. Laura sat down and started reading it. After a few moments she got up to find a pen.

"Don't scribble on that," her mother said as she came into the kitchen.

Laura looked at her mother. She opened her mouth to speak, then decided not to bother. It could take years for Laura to work out how to have a conversation with her mother, a proper conversation with volleys like a game of tennis. Or she might never work it out. She knew from her newspapers that there were many things she couldn't comprehend. Even though her mother wasn't a treaty or a war or a disease, she was complex and it wasn't possible to understand her by looking her up in an encyclopaedia.

Laura put the pen down and went into the lounge. Her father was sitting in his armchair eating toast and Marmite and watching *Countdown*. Lisa was sitting on the floor with her back against her father's armchair.

"Dad, you need to take your CV back to the computer at the job centre and make some changes." Laura walked over to his chair and handed him the sheets of paper. "I've found some spelling mistakes and you haven't mentioned your voluntary work on the cricket club committee or that shed you helped build for Lisa's Brownies. And you could say a lot more about your old job. I've put down some suggestions."

Her father read her notes and looked up at her. He had a crumb of toast in the corner of his mouth. "Thanks, love.

You're such a clever girl, I don't know how we managed to come up with you. Or you," he added, ruffling Lisa's hair.

"HAVING A CLEAR-OUT HERE TOO?" Victoria said.

Laura took her head out of the locker. "I was early so I thought I'd have a sort-out before Sonia gets here. I'm sick of her hogging the locker."

Victoria sat down on the floor and crossed her legs.

"Look what I found." Laura dangled a knotted tangle of hair and dust in front of Victoria's face.

Victoria leaned away, grimacing.

"No, look. It's my necklace. I found it in the bottom of the locker. The locker louts didn't steal it after all."

"Make sure you wash all that locker lout crap off it before you wear it," Victoria said. "Hey, I've got something else for you."

She took a roll of paper and some tape out of her bag and stood up. It was one of the pictures of British Columbia from the magazine. "Hope you don't mind me cutting it out. Did you know there are twice as many people in Britain than in Canada but Canada is thirty-eight times bigger?"

Laura pretended she didn't know. "That's amazing," she said.

"There are twenty-eight million, three hundred and seventy-seven thousand people in Canada." Victoria paused to bite off a piece of tape. "Here, there are fifty-seven million, six hundred thousand. No wonder it feels so bloody crowded." She stuck the top of the picture to the door, then bit off another piece of tape and stuck it along the bottom. "If the locker louts rip it out, we'll get another one. I've written off for some brochures. I think we should save up and go to Canada after our A levels. Okay?"

"Sure," Laura said.

Victoria grabbed Laura's shoulders and turned her so they were facing each other. "I mean it," Victoria said. "Okay?"

The stern look on Victoria's face made Laura laugh. "Okay,"

she said. "I mean it too."

It was the picture of a turquoise lake in front of steep mountains. The sky was a blue that came from purple while the turquoise was a blue that came from green. Laura didn't think it was possible for the sky and a lake to be such different colours. Water was colourless; it always reflected the sky.

After school, Laura cycled down to the beach and stood on the promenade with her legs astride her bicycle. The sea was aluminum grey and the sky was the off-white of an old towel. When you thought about it, it was obvious. Of course sky and sea could be different colours. Air and water were different elements.

Laura leant her bike against the railings and ran down to the edge of the sand. She untied her shoes and stuffed her socks into them, then waded into the water. Her feet started to throb from the cold. She carefully removed the triskelion necklace from her pocket. A triskelion represented three elements. Water for sharks, air for humans. She took a deep breath. Breathing was easy. The third element must be land. Land was the element she wasn't used to yet. When she was older, she would visit other countries and find one where she didn't feel so out of place.

She leaned forward and, holding the chain tightly in her fist, she dipped the necklace into the sea.

Acknowledgements

THANK YOU TO PAUL WILSON AND TINA DMYTRYSHYN AT Hagios Press for their belief in this collection. I am very grateful that curtains are being drawn back, lights are being switched on, and the characters in these stories are stirring and waking once more.

Versions of many of these stories were first published in anthologies and journals in Scotland, England, and Canada, for which I am thankful. "The Accents of Birds" was published in *The Scotsman* and Orange Short Story Award *Secrets* collection (Polygon); "Manniit" was published in *A Fictional Guide to Scotland* (OpenInk) and "Perhaps Birches" was published in *The Final Theory and Other Stories* (Leaf Books).

"Magnetic North" was published in *Pushing Out The Boat*, "Silver Salmon" was published in *The Eildon Tre*, and "The World's First Spin Doctor" was published in *Ironstone*. "Machair" was published in *QWF*, a journal to which I am especially thankful for encouraging me to keep trying. "Death on the Wing" was published in *Delivered*.

In Canada, "The Birthday Books" and "Rearranging Rainbows" were published in *Grain*, and "Travelling Light" was published in *All Rights Reserved*. "The Birthday Books" was a finalist for *The Malahat Review* Open Season Awards, "Rearranging Rainbows" was a finalist for *The Malahat Review*

Far Horizon Award for Short Fiction, and "Carbonated" was a finalist for The Writers" Union of Canada Short Prose Competition.

I am indebted to Zoë Wicomb, my tutor for my MLitt in Creative Writing at the Universities of Glasgow and Strathclyde, for helping me develop my craft and encouraging me to believe my work might be worthy of publication. I also thank Patricia Robertson and Laura Hutchinson for their insights and for their enthusiasm for the short story. And thank you to Lily Gontard for reminding me that a short story collection can never be published if it is never submitted.

Writing is a necessarily self-absorbed pastime and most of all I thank my husband, Glenn Rudman, for donating so much of our time together to my individual cause.

MARTIN BERKMAN

Joanna Lilley is an award-wining writer who has lived in Whitehorse, Yukon, since she emigrated from the UK in 2006. Her poetry collection, *The Fleece Era*, was published by Brick Books in 2014. Joanna's poems and stories have been published in journals and anthologies in Canada, the US and the UK, including *The Malahat Review, The New Quarterly, Grain, The Fiddlehead,* and *The Antigonish Review.* Joanna has a MLitt degree in creative writing from the universities of Glasgow and Strathclyde, and is a Humber School for Writers graduate. In 2011 and 2013, she received Advanced Artist Awards from the Government of Yukon. With diplomas in plain language editing and journalism, Joanna earns her living as a public sector communications professional.